the
Grand
Plan
to Fix
Everything

Also by Uma Krishnaswami

The Problem with Being Slightly Heroic

the Grand Plan to Fix Everything

by Uma Krishnaswami

illustrated by Abigail Halpin

 ATHENEUM BOOKS FOR YOUNG READERS

New York London Toronto Sydney New Delhi

A
atheneum

ATHENEUM BOOKS FOR YOUNG READERS

An imprint of Simon & Schuster Children's Publishing Division

1230 Avenue of the Americas, New York, New York 10020

This book is a work of fiction. Any references to historical events, real people, or real places are used fictitiously. Other names, characters, places, and events are products of the author's imagination, and any resemblance to actual events or places or persons, living or dead, is entirely coincidental.

Text copyright © 2011 by Uma Krishnaswami

Illustrations copyright © 2011 by Abigail Halpin

All rights reserved, including the right of reproduction in whole or in part in any form.

ATHENEUM BOOKS FOR YOUNG READERS is a registered trademark of Simon & Schuster, Inc. Atheneum logo is a trademark of Simon & Schuster, Inc.

For information about special discounts for bulk purchases, please contact Simon & Schuster Special Sales at 1-866-506-1949 or business@simonandschuster.com.

The Simon & Schuster Speakers Bureau can bring authors to your live event. For more information or to book an event, contact the Simon & Schuster Speakers Bureau at 1-866-248-3049 or visit our website at www.simonspeakers.com.

Also available in an Atheneum Books for Young Readers hardcover edition

Book design by Debra Sfetsios-Conover

The text for this book is set in Centaur.

The illustrations for this book are rendered in pen and ink.

Manufactured in the United States of America

0515 OFF

First Atheneum Books for Young Readers paperback edition February 2013

10 9 8 7 6 5 4 3 2

Krishnaswami, Uma, 1956–

The grand plan to fix everything / Uma Krishnaswami ;

[illustrations by Abigail Halpin]. — 1st ed.

p. cm.

Summary: Eleven-year-old Dini loves movies, and so when she learns that her family is moving to India for two years, her devastation over leaving her best friend in Maryland is tempered by the possibility of meeting her favorite actress, Dolly Singh.

ISBN 978-1-4169-9589-0 (hc)

[1. Best friends—Fiction. 2. Friendship—Fiction. 3. Actors and actresses—Fiction. 4. East Indian Americans—Fiction. 5. Moving, Household—Fiction. 6. India—Fiction.]

I. Halpin, Abigail, ill. II. Title.

PZ7.K8975Gr 2011

[Fic]—dc22

2010035145

ISBN 978-1-4169-9590-6 (paperback)

ISBN 978-1-4169-9591-3 (eBook)

For my parents, V.K. and Vasantha,

who brought me home to the original Sunny Villa

A freshly baked curry puff of gratitude to all those who helped me get a grip on Dini's story: Tobin Anderson, Kathi Appelt, Stephanie Farrow, Lucy Hampson, Katherine Hauth, Vaunda Micheaux Nelson, and Rosemary Stimola. May the kurinji flower bloom for you all. Thanks to my students at writers.com who kept me on my toes: Nandini Bajpai, Lanita Dawson-Jones, Annette Gulati, Kiki Hamilton, Rani Iyer, Lindsey Lane, Ann McDonald, Paula McLaughlin, and Tina Shannon. I'll dance with you all on any rooftop you choose. Sumant and Nikhil, you get the chocolate cake. Students and fellow faculty members at Vermont College of Fine Arts, thank you for listening to me read and reread from this when it was still as drafty as Noble Hall in January. Thanks to members of Sawnet, who sent me lists of Hindi movies so I could learn to think like a true fan. To Vicki Holmsten and Bisti Writing Project. To Erica Stahler, heroic copy editor, for untangling the story's chronology. To Kiley Frank, who stepped in time with Dolly. Finally, Caitlyn Dlouhy, you are my shining star. May your mail arrive on time, lovingly delivered, and may monkeys stay out of your water-tank.

Chapter One

MJTJ

DOLLY SINGH'S FABULOUS FACE FLOATS across the screen of the TV in the family room. Two happy sighs float off the couch, one from Dini and the other from her best friend, Maddie.

Dini is a Dolly fan. She has been forever, from the time she discovered that Dolly's first movie, in which she was just a kid, came out the day—the very day!—that Dini was born. You can't be more closely connected than that.

Maddie is a fan because best friends share everything.

Closer and closer comes Dolly's face, until her hair turns to mist and the sunlight catches her brown gold skin. Dolly opens her mouth to sing a perfectly tuneful song in this, her latest movie, *Mera jeevan tera jeevan*, or *My Life Your Life*, MJTJ for short. Dini and Maddie sing along, tapping their feet and dropping from the words into quick little "la-la-la's" whenever they have to.

"Dolly is sooooo . . . ," Dini says.

"She is," Maddie agrees. "She's sooooo . . ."

So smart. So elegant. So talented. So perfect. Other stars must rely on lip-synching and playback singers. Not Dolly. Dolly can act. She can dance as if her feet were on fire. *And* she can sing.

"I'd love to *meet* her," Maddie says. "Wouldn't that be awesome?"

"Oh wow," says Dini. Not much else to say. She tap-taps her feet in a moment of pure delight. "You know what I love about Dolly?"

"Everything!" says Maddie, throwing her arms wide in that special Dolly way.

"Oh yeah, but you want to know specially what?" She has just this moment realized this thing about Dolly. "When she says stuff, people listen!"

"Except the bad guys," Maddie points out, "and we know what happens to them."

"Must be nice to say stuff and have people listen," Dini says.

"Dini," Maddie tells her. "I will always listen to you. Anytime."

"I know that," Dini says. "I meant—you know, parents and people."

"Oh. Parents," says Maddie.

It's true. Parents do seem to exist just to complicate the life of a kid. Dini's parents, for example, are not fans. They laugh at the sad parts in the movies and groan at the funny ones, even though they are from India, where Dolly lives, and they should know better.

"Oh-oh-oh, listen!" Dini says. "Here comes that amazing song."

"Sunno-sunno," Dolly sings, right into their hearts, "dekho-dekho."

Dini listen-listens. She look-looks. And here is the best part. Maddie is doing exactly the same thing. Two friends together, sharing this wonderful music. What could be better?

Many people love Bollywood movies from India. They are made in the city of Bombay, which is now really called Mumbai, only filmi people like Dini still call it by the old name because it's classier. The dialogue in these movies is all in Hindi, but you can get them with subtitles in languages from Arabic to French to Thai because so many people all over the world are fans, just like Dini and Maddie.

"I can't wait for dance camp," Dini says.

"I know, me neither," Maddie says. "It'll be soooo . . ."

Maddie's parents are not from India, and Maddie understands even less Hindi than Dini does, but little things like language don't get in the way of a really good fillum, which is what true fans affectionately call these movies. Fillums. In just another month Dini and Maddie will be in that camp for a whole two weeks of Bollywood dance—what a treat that will be.

Chan-chan-chan, go Dolly's silver anklets.

Dhoom-taana-dhoom, go the drumbeats.

Dini and Maddie watch MJTJ from start to finish, snapping their fingers and tapping their feet. Then they watch the special features, with interviews and bios of everyone from the camera people to the director to the stars, including, of course, Dolly herself.

"Wait-wait-wait," Dini says, "go back just a bit."

"What? To the interview?" Maddie hits the back arrow on the remote. "Hey, they're talking in English." A TV reporter is interviewing Dolly and asking her for her opinion on the latest trends in Hindi movies.

"It's surreal what's happening in the movie business," Dolly is saying. "Surreal, I tell you."

"What's that mean?" Maddie says. "Surreal?"

Dini shakes her head. "Real" she gets, and "unreal." But "surreal"? What's that? "I'll ask my dad," she says. Dad is her vocabulary consultant for the Hindi words and sometimes a few English ones too.

Playing the interview over is not much help. Dolly says that the Bombay movie business is becoming that surreal thing, whatever it is.

"She doesn't seem happy," Dini says. "What do you think?"

"You're right," Maddie agrees. True fans can pick up on even the tiniest of cues.

"Nandu!" It's Mom. "Are you upstairs? Listen, sweetoo, I have news for you." Dini wishes her parents would not call her Nandu. In their time, in the last century, that was how you shortened Dini's real name, which is Nandini.

Mom comes in with a handful of mail (including the latest copy of *Filmi Kumpnee* magazine). "Hi,

Maddie, I didn't know you were here. Nandu, guess what? I just got the contract in the mail. Such wonderful news."

What contract? What news? Dini pauses Dolly with a click so she can listen to whatever boring thing Mom is about to tell her.

Mom puts the new *Filmi Kumpnee* into Dini's outstretched hand. "We're moving to India," she says.

Chapter Two

Moving

DINI DROPS THE MAGAZINE. "Mom," she says. "I know you didn't just say that we're moving to India, but it sounded like it."

Mom grabs Dini and hugs her. She dances Dini around Maddie in a wobbly circle, saying, "Oh darlings, what can I say? I'm soooo happy!"

This is not at all like Mom, because Mom is a doctor. Doctors are supposed to be serious and thoughtful and all those kinds of things, not act like they are out of their mind.

"You mean it, don't you?" Dini says. "Moving?"

"We are, we are, we are!" Mom cries. "For two years. Isn't it wonderful?" Then she stops, as if she has only just seen Dini's face, only just heard her voice. "I know," she says. "It's going to take you a little time to get used to the idea. We still have a couple of weeks."

And there is Maddie's face. Can't Mom see that Maddie has frozen in staring shock? "Mom!" Dini cries. "A couple of weeks? What about Bollywood dance camp?"

"Oh, sweetie," says Mom in the kind of voice that parents use when they are trying to be sympathetic but they really want to say that kid-size problems are not real problems.

Maddie's chin quivers. She looks about to burst into tears. Dini herself is dangerously close.

India is where Dini and her family go on vacation to visit relatives, because according to Dad, there is no such thing as a distant one. India is where you see cool places and take trains everywhere, and eat mangoes and custard apples and other fun food. Vacations last for a couple of weeks, or maybe even a whole month. But two years?

Mom is dancing around the room by herself now, picking a leaf green scarf out of the old dress-up basket in the corner.

Maddie is flipping through the pages of the *Filmi Kumpnee* magazine without seeming to look at anything. "Maybe you'll get to meet Dolly," she says in a small, brave voice.

"I doubt it," says Dini. "India's a big country. Really big." That sounds like she's shooting down Maddie's idea, and it's not at all how she meant it to sound. Maddie's only trying to be helpful. Maddie's only trying.

Mom folds the green scarf, which has silver flowery designs stamped on it. She folds it in two and then four and then eight and then sixteen, and she's still folding. Dini snatches the scarf from Mom's hands because Mom is not responsible for her actions right now, and that is one of Dini's favorite scarves.

"How do you know . . . until you try?" Maddie says, and this time her words crack right in the middle.

"Exactly," says Mom, who obviously can't understand anything. "I've dreamed of getting this grant for years and years. This is my sixth try, imagine that." And she goes on about clinics and women and children and studies and weight gain, all of which seems to make her very happy.

The TV screen has given up on Dolly's face and has dissolved into a swirly multicolored screen saver.

"Mom," Dini says, and it's all she can do to keep her own voice from swirling away from her, "where's this place you're—we're . . ." She can't quite say it. It's not quite real. It's probably miles away from Bombay, the center of the filmi universe, and what does it matter anyway? Regular people don't get to meet movie stars, no matter how much they may adore them and want to be like them in every possible way.

Mom stops in the middle of picking up a silk blouse that is now just a little too small for Dini. She sets the blouse down in Dini's old dress-up basket.

Then she picks the globe off the shelf, and she spins it to India and stops it with a little squeak of the Earth's axis. "That's where we're going." She points. "It's a little town called Swapnagiri."

Dini looks at Maddie. Maddie looks at Dini.

"That means 'dream mountain,'" Mom says. "Isn't that a wonderful name?"

Dini says nothing. The dream of that Bollywood dance camp fades way away into the distance. As for that other dream, the meeting-Dolly dream . . .

Doctors are supposed to be both practical and kind, and Mom is a doctor. So she does not say, "This Dream Mountain place may be in the same country as Bombay, the center of the filmi universe, but it is not close. Not close at all. So all this talk about meeting Dolly—as the gossip columns would say, it's just bakvaas."

Mom, being both kind and practical, does not say that. Mom would never say, "This dream of yours is all bakvaas." But looking at the globe, Dini can see it.

The day goes by in a flurry of no-no-no and how-can-this-be-happening. Maddie goes home to pick up her pajamas and toothbrush and backpack, but she's coming back to spend the night at Dini's, so they can take the bus to school together the following day. Maddie's mom has agreed to this, on account of this move that has dropped out of the sky on two friends.

Dini tries to talk to her vocabulary consultant (that is to say, Dad) when he gets home from work, but Mom has called him already with her big news, and for a while after he walks in the door, it is all that they can talk about. Dini has to wait for the drama to die down all over again before she can get a word in sideways.

She hangs in there, however, and eventually she gets to ask, "Dad, what does 'surreal' mean?"

"'Bizarre,'" Dad says, handing something small and shiny to Mom. "Like a dream. As they say, out of the ordinary, beyond the pale." Whenever he can, Dad likes to use nifty phrases like these, phrases that sum things up neatly.

"What's this?" Mom says, looking at the shiny thing.

"A hand-cranked flashlight with a radio all in one," says Gadget Dad, looking very pleased with himself. "Twenty cranks will power it for five minutes."

"Is that good or bad?" says Dini.

"Of course it's good. No batteries. The ultimate green gadget, my darlings. Perfect timing, no? Things like this are always useful in India."

"No, no, no," Dini says. "I meant what Dolly says the filmi business is becoming, surreal or whatever it is."

"That," says Dad in between showing Mom how the flashlight has three settings and a radio and can probably be trained to make coffee, "sounds like a complaint."

So it's bad.

Chapter Three

Maddie

PLINKA-PLINK! There's the musical doorbell announcing that Maddie's back with all of her stuff. Maddie's mom, who has driven her over, has a long talk with Dini's mom. They talk in low voices. Dini can't think why, because who would even want to hear?

After dinner Dini and Maddie paint their toenails because that always makes them feel better. Every other nail, green and silver, Dolly's colors. Then they sit on the couch wiggling their toes dry and run through the MJTJ special features all over again.

"Haven't you seen this one already?" Mom asks.

"Please," Dini begs. "Mom, just one more time."

Mom gives in. She leaves them alone.

First they run through the scenes, one by one by one. Then they listen to the songs, comparing them with the list in Dini's stripy green notebook,

where she has written down each Hindi title and its meaning in English.

Really, Dolly is all the things that Dini admires in a person, all the things that Dini absolutely means to be at some time in the future when her life becomes perfect. Which it is not right now, most definitely.

"I wish this Swapnagiri place was closer," says Dini. She means closer to here, in Maryland. Or maybe closer to Bombay. She's not sure what she means.

"I know," says Maddie. Maddie gets it. No one else does.

Dini flips a moody page. Look at all the movie ideas she has written down in her stripy notebook. Who is she going to share them with if Maddie's not there?

They do not hum along with the songs or *dhoom-dhoom* the drumbeats because any minute Mom could change her mind and declare that it is way too late for them to be up watching Dolly. Instead, they fast-forward through scenes where she runs over bridges and down city streets, rounds up bad guys and locks them up. Watching these scenes should make Maddie happy, but they don't. Oh, this move is going to ruin everything!

Then Dini clicks the DVD to a stop. "Wait a minute," she says. "Something's wrong."

"What?" Maddie says. "What are you talking about?"

Dini goes to the menu with the list of songs. She taps the open pages of her notebook. Dini's Hindi is not great, but she has made Consultant Dad do his job. "Facing the music," he calls it. Dini has made him tell her what the songs mean from title through lyrics, every single one.

Now those meanings are whirling about in her mind. What is each song really about? What is it saying? And she knows. Something is wrong.

Dini is a big believer in talking. Talking helps you to solve problems whenever you can. It's what filmi people call a "plot fix." She says, "You know how in every movie she's ever done there are happy songs and sad songs?"

"Right," Maddie says. "So?"

"This new movie," says Dini, "has no happy songs."

"Huh?"

"Uh-huh. Look at this."

She reads off all the English translations of the song titles to Maddie: "If I Call You, Will You Come?" "No One Knows Where My House Is," "Only Clear Skies Will Cure a Broken Heart," and on and on.

"See?" she says. "Not a single happy one. No running in the forest in the rain. No scattering flowers. Not a happy song in there."

Maddie slides off the couch and heel-walks to the table, keeping her toenails carefully off the rug. She picks up the *Filmi Kumpnee* magazine. Then she heel-walks back, falls onto the couch, and opens the magazine up between them. "Let's see," she says. "We never looked at this."

She's right. The news of the day distracted them from this very important thing they should have done together. Dini and Maddie pore over the *Filmi Kumpnee* magazine, which keeps up with everything the stars do. There is the page with Dolly's happy, smiley pictures on it. But those pictures must have been taken some time ago, because the article on the page is not a bit happy and smiley.

From the "News 'n' Views" column of *Filmi Kumpnee: Your Magazine of the Stars*:

Devoted Dolly Singh fans, we have News 'n'
Views for you. Our own inside sources tell us
that delightful Dolly is on the verge of . . .

She is on the brink of . . .

Oh, how it hurts us even to think of it, but
the word is:

Heartbreak.

You are so sorry, we know.

We are too. That is all we can reveal at this
moment. But we are ever alert. You be alert
also. Watch this spot for the latest additions
to this stunning story.

"Heartbreak?" says Maddie. "That's terrible."

"I know!" says Dini. Then she shares this idea
that has been bubbling up inside her ever since that
"surreal" word cropped up. "Maddie, I'm going to
write her. What do you think?"

"Dolly?" says Maddie. "Do you even have her
address?"

A stubborn spark lights up in Dini. She says,

"She's famous. I'm just going to send my letter to Dolly Singh, Famous Movie Star, Bombay, India."

"Will it get there?"

"Why not?" says Dini. "Everyone in Bombay has to know Dolly Singh."

Maddie considers this seriously. Then she says, in a small voice, "I wish I could come to India with you. I bet two of us could find a way to meet Dolly."

"Oh, Maddie," says Dini, and she hugs her, and they both cry a little and get tissues to blow their noses. This is a thing that no one ever needs to do in the movies, but real life can require a good blowing of the nose sometimes.

Dini says, "Maybe you can come visit us."

"In India?" Maddie gives her a look that says, plain as plain, Are you crazy?

"Why not?" says Dini. A big, wide expanse of why-not opens up inside her. Perhaps this is because Dini is an optimist, and optimists are always open to such why-nots. A bit like Dolly in MJTJ. Or perhaps it is just that when you are moving (a little reluctantly, true, but still, moving) to a place whose name means "dream mountain," your mind begins to open up in strange ways, so that anything really does seem possible.

May 31, 2010

Dear Dolly Singh,

My name is Nandini Kumaran, but my friends call me Dini. I am a big fan of yours, and my friend Maddie is too. We were even going to take Bollywood dance camp together in Greenbelt, Maryland, only now we can't because my parents are moving to India for two whole years.

I have a VERY important QUESTION for you. I noticed that there are no happy songs in MJTJ. You always do at least one in every movie. So is that a screen appeal decision or is it something else? I just want to know that you are okay.

We are going to be in the south,
up in some mountains, in a town
called Swapnagiri. If you come visit
us, that would be like a dream come
true for me.

Your fan and friend,

Dini

Chapter Four

Dream Mountain

THE BLUE MOUNTAINS RISE unexpectedly out of the hot land of south India. Their misty heights are covered with forests and green bursts of tea-gardens; little towns hide among their hilly pleats and folds.

One of those towns is called Swapnagiri.

At first glance Swapnagiri may seem like a long name, with lots of letters all racing after each other, just the way the cars and buses race along the winding mountain roads.

But to that open-minded person who sounds the name out, one letter at a time, it falls quite handily into place: S-w-a-p-n-a-g-i-r-i. An honest sort of name, with no surprise letters waiting to leap out and ambush the unwary. It is what it is.

And yes, this is that very same place, far from Bombay, the center of the filmi universe. The place to which Dini and her parents are about to make their way.

Swapnagiri. Dream Mountain.

Sometimes names stick to places for very good reasons.

Chapter Five

Take Note

THE MORNING AFTER MOM'S big announcement Dini peels an airmail stamp off the sheet of them that Dad keeps in the kitchen drawer. She sticks it on the envelope she's addressed to Dolly. Then she sticks an extra one on, just to be sure. She and Maddie drop the letter into the mailbox on the corner before they catch the bus to school.

"How long will it take?" Maddie asks.

"I think about a week," Dini says. She crosses her fingers and toes as she says it, because you never know.

At school that day the news of the Move gets around fast. Everyone seems to think that it will be a wonderful adventure. Dini tries to

hang with Maddie all day because Maddie's the only person who understands how she feels.

Dini wants to go. To find Dolly. To find out what's wrong with Dolly. To tell Maddie everything she finds out.

At the same time, she wants to stay. Stay. Go. Stay. Go. It is as if she has one arm stretching toward India and Dolly, and one arm right here, and she is going to be pulled in two.

Two years is a long time. By the end of the school day, after explaining over and over that she's going to be living in India for two years, and duh, she will not be riding an elephant to school, Dini's exhausted. But she's also beginning to get just a tiny bit excited. There is that push-pull again.

"Can I go to Maddie's?" Dini asks as soon as she has finished dashing through her homework that afternoon.

"Wasn't she just here last night?" Dad asks. "And you were with her in school all day too?"

"Yes, but can I go?"

He looks at Mom. Mom shrugs and smiles. "Sure, why not?" Mom is making lists of things to do, things to sell, lists of airline itineraries, lists of people who may want to rent their house for a couple of years. Mom is so busy that if Dini asked for permission to ride her bike to the moon, Mom would probably shrug and smile and say, "Why not?"

"Come back before it gets dark," Dad says as he helps Dini get her bike out of the garage.

"Okay."

Dini pedals her way down the street and heads two blocks over to Maddie's house.

Maddie is wiping down a big reusable magnetic sheet stuck to the fridge door in her kitchen. "My mom gave me this old calendar," she says. "We can draw in it every day. Until. You know."

"Oh, Maddie," says Dini.

"When?" Maddie says. "Do you have a date yet?"

"Nope," Dini says. "Mom's checking out airline schedules, and they're trying to rent a house."

"There?"

"Yup. And get someone to rent ours."

"Here," says Maddie. It has a final sort of sound.

"And stuff," Dini ends lamely.

"Okay," says Maddie, pulling the cap off an erasable marker with a flourish. "We'll just fill up the ones we need. Here's today—Tuesday, June first. You want to start?"

Dini hesitates, then accepts the green marker. She draws a star.

"Nice," Maddie says. She draws a rectangle with squiggles on it six, no seven, squares down.

"What's that?" Dini asks.

"Silly," Maddie says, "it's your letter. Flying into Dolly's hands. I gave it an extra day, just in case."

Dini hugs Maddie so hard that Maddie says, "Yikes. Eep. Ouch," and they laugh together because that is how friends are.

Chapter Six

No PIN Code?

CHAAP! CHAAP! CHAAP! The sorting machine in a post office in Mumbai, India (used to be called Bombay), stamps the letters. The postmaster himself supervises the emptying of bags into the machine. There are bags from Delhi. There is one from Kolkata. There are bags from Bangalore and Kochi and many other places all over India. Bags from Switzerland and Zimbabwe and Australia. And from the United States of America.

The workers empty the bag from Delhi. They empty the bags from Kolkata and all the other cities and countries.

The bags from the United States are big and full. The postmaster himself has to help lift them up. "Careful," he warns. "These are not sacks of potatoes, but valuable foreign mail!"

A letter falls from one of the United States bags.

It falls onto the floor. The postmaster picks it up.

"What? No PIN code?" barks the postmaster. "How does this foolish person think we can find this . . . let me see"—he peers through his glasses at the address—"this Dolly Singh. How can we find her without a *PIN code*?"

The post office workers joke and laugh, and say mean things about the silly person from America who didn't know about the number codes that every proper address should have. Not one of them dares to point out that the postmaster is just plain ignorant about the fillums. In fact, it is quite remarkable that he has never heard of Dolly Singh, but that could be because he is a very senior postmaster and therefore not interested in the fads and follies of the young.

"P-please, sir?" stammers a voice. It is the newest, youngest postal worker. His name is Lal and he has been on this job all of six months. His clothes crackle eagerly from the starch his mother puts in the rinsing water.

Lal is only a lowly postal carrier, whose job is to ride his bicycle along the streets of Mumbai, taking the mail to people's doors and putting it in the right boxes. He has ventured into this august sorting room only because his bicycle bell has recently lost its tinkle. The postmaster must sign a form so that Lal can get a new bell.

Lal pushes his form timidly at the postmaster, who grabs it from him and looks menacingly at it.

"Please, s-sir," says Lal. "D-did I hear you m-mention D-dolly S-singh the m-movie star, sir?"

The postmaster is so shocked that Lal has dared to speak without being spoken to that he signs the form and hands it right back. "Movie shoovie, all bakvaas," growls the postmaster.

Lal trembles, but he says, "I know w-w-where she lives. It's on m-m-my route." Because Lal is a Dolly Singh fan. He loves her movies, all of them. He hums the songs as he delivers the mail. And while he is careful to deliver all the mail with speed and efficiency (per the India Post motto), he always drops Dolly's mail into her box with crackly-swift speed and efficiency.

"She should tell her friends," grumbles the postmaster, "about PIN codes! What does she think, this is some tin-pot place without postal regulations?"

But he hands the letter to Lal. "Bombay!" he mutters. "Couldn't even get the name right. All right, all right. Off with you, my man."

Lal sneaks a look at the envelope. He sees it has been date-stamped "June 1" in some place called Takoma Park, Maryland, far away in the United States of America.

Today is the eighth. This letter has taken exactly a week to get more than halfway around the world. What a fine thing a properly working postal system is.

By now the machine has *chaap-chaap-chaaped* all the mail and dumped it into bags that slide out all by themselves to the place where the carriers can pick them up for delivery. Such are the wonders of technology.

Lal hefts his bag off the conveyor belt and over his shoulder. Off he goes, stopping only at the supply department to turn in his form and get his new bell. Then he carries his big, bulging bag out to his bicycle. He disconnects the old broken bell and fixes the new one in its place. *Trrring!* It has a nice musical sound. He loads up and sets off.

On his way Lal hums a little song, his favorite

one from his favorite Dolly Singh movie. He *trrrings* his new bell to let people know when he is making a left turn or a right turn or even sometimes for no reason at all. He is happy that he rescued this letter for Dolly, because he thinks perhaps this letter is from someone who is also a fan. Fans sometimes do crazy things like mailing letters even when they don't know the proper address.

Sometimes the universe bends its rules a little for people who really need to get in touch with other people. The thing that everyone calls coincidence— well, Lal thinks it may be more than that. Coincidence is big in the fillums Lal loves, and he is never happier than when life occasionally imitates a really good fillum.

When he gets to the building, which is ground-floor-plus-ten-floors high, he takes all his letters and drops them carefully into the correct boxes. He drops the Dolly Singh letter even more carefully into its correct box. It is very full, that Dolly box. She needs to check her mail, he thinks. Those fans will be waiting.

Then out of the lobby and back onto his bike goes Lal, a happy young man doing a good day's work.

Chapter Seven

Coming Apart

DINI'S ROOM IS COMING APART like a bad plot. Dini and Maddie are curled up under the desk, which has been turned into a tent by throwing a comforter over it, since everything else on the desk has now been packed, stored, or given away.

Dini and Maddie have not built one of these furniture tents since they were in second grade together, but these are desperate times. "They found a renter," Dini says.

"For here? This house?"

"Mmm."

"What about your stuff?"

"The furniture's going to stay here and the drapes and things. Some of it's in storage. Jiji Auntie—Mom's sister—is going to keep our car. Until we get back." Two years from now. It might as well be two centuries.

Maddie says, "I brought you something." She gives Dini a glittery green gel pen to go with her green stripy notebook from the green stripy Dolly collection.

"Oh, Maddie," says Dini. "Thank you." And suddenly, in her empty room, with the Dolly poster rolled up and the shelves empty of books and games and pictures, the distance yawns wide as oceans between Takoma Park, Maryland, and Swapnagiri that means Dream Mountain.

"Seven days," Dini says.

"That means it must have gotten there by now," Maddie says.

"I don't know," says Dini, who is now assailed by doubts. Like waves on some fillum beach, these doubts. They wash over her when she's not expecting them. What was she thinking? How foolish to have sent a letter off without a proper address and expect that it would get there.

But Maddie will not give up. "I bet she replies right away," says Maddie. "So then seven days for the reply to come back, and you'll still get her letter before. You know."

Before you leave. On June 16.

They still can't say it, either of them. The leaving part has sunk in, of course, with eight more days to go, but in between America and India they're now in best-friend country, where some things don't need to be said and others can't bear to be.

School will be out in a few more days. Dini has said her good-byes to a lot of people, but not to Maddie. Not yet.

"You have to think positive," Maddie says. "Dolly would think positive. You have to think, 'WWDD?'"

"What?" What's that? Some new movie Dini has not heard of?

Maddie grins at her in the light that is filtering lavender and blue through the patterns of the comforter. "'What Would Dolly Do,' silly," she says.

Dini breathes deeply. "You're right." It's true. Dolly is big on thinking positive. In MJTJ when Dolly is on a cliff, hanging on for dear life, she thinks positive. Thinking positive helps her to remember that she has a cell phone in

her pocket with the TV station's number on the speed-dial list, and so she is able to call for help right when you'd think there were no choices left.

"Maddie," Dini says. "I know this is going to sound crazy."

Maddie makes sympathetic go-on-and-tell-me-anyway noises.

"I figure," Dini says, "that even if Swapnagiri is far from Bombay . . ."

"The center of the filmi universe," they proclaim together.

"It's still closer to it than Takoma Park, Maryland. So I should really try to get in touch with Dolly. And I will. Because look." And Dini shows Maddie this week's issue of *Filmi Kumpnee*.

From the "News 'n' Views" column of *Filmi Kumpnee: Your Magazine of the Stars*:

Dolly Singh fans, take note. Our hardworking, scoop-finding *Filmi Kumpnee* reporters have news for you. Nothing less than word from Soli Dustup himself. Yes, that Soli Dustup—manager, owner, and artistic director of Bombay's own Starlite Studios.

And the word is—silence.

Yes, that's right. Our beautiful and fabulous and always-happy-to-talk Dolly Singh is Giving No Interviews.

"What-what-what?" you may ask. "Why not?" We asked too. Soliji's mum on the what and the why. But Dolly, it seems, is indeed not talking. No TV, no radio, not even *Filmi Kumpnee*'s own tireless reporters can wangle an interview.

Mysterious indeed. Is it love, we wonder, that has made our dazzling Dolly fall silent? Will there be a new movie? "No comment," says Mr. Soli Dustup.

We are ever alert. You be alert too. Keep your eye on this column.

"Maddie," says Dini. "I promise you that the minute I find Dolly—the minute—I will let you know."

"By e-mail?" Maddie says.

"Maddie," Dini says. "E-mail or mail or phone or text or whatever."

"Maybe if you even just think hard enough, I'll hear your thoughts," Maddie says.

"I'll think," Dini promises. "I'll think so loud and long and hard I bet it'll wake you up."

"Send me jokes."

"And songs."

"How about video? You think you can thought-send video?"

"Dance steps?"

They laugh so hard that Dini's parents peek in to make sure they are not crying. Sometimes it is hard to tell the difference.

"Those two have really become glued together," Dini hears her dad say.

"Velcroed," says Mom. "Can't say I blame them."

Chapter Eight

Fan Letters

IN MUMBAI THAT ALL THE FILMI
people still insist on calling Bombay, in the hallway
of a twelfth-floor apartment that for some strange
reason is called a flat, Mr. Soli Dustup of Starlite
Studios is on the telephone.

Sometimes, as the best filmi people know, nothing works like snappy dialogue. This is why Mr.
Dustup has been making phone call after phone
call to a certain person. But you can't have any dialogue, snappy or otherwise, when the other person
refuses to answer the phone.

And the fan mail! "Soli, do me a favor and take
care of the fan mail for me," she said, dropping
off the key before taking off on this jaunt to some
hilly place no one has ever heard of. "Just use this
letter—only till I get back, there's a good chap."
And she thrust a signed "Dearest Friend and Fan"

letter into his hand, typed on that creamy stationery she likes to use.

"No blinking problem, Dolly darling," he replied. He groans now to think of it. He should have asked her then: "Where are you going? When will you be back? Exactly how long will I have to answer your blinking fan letters?"

In silent exasperation he shakes his fist at temperamental movie stars who just pick up whenever they want to and go off to parts unknown without a thought for their producers, directors, studio executives—and fans!

Mr. Soli Dustup thinks sadly, You should look before you leap, Dolly darling. Looking before she leaps has never been Dolly's strong suit.

Chapter Nine

A Sign

SCHOOL IS OUT AT LAST. The calendar has moved into Dini's room. So has Maddie.

Dini and Maddie are going to spend every last hour and minute together until. You know.

"Two days and—when did you say your flight was?" Maddie says.

"Ten o'clock at night," Dini says. "From Baltimore, which means we have to leave here at six p.m."

"That means two days and . . ." Maddie is making little marks for hours and minutes on the edge of the calendar, being careful not to smudge the stars and houses and letters and butterflies and birds that are scattered all over it already. "No, no, I'm wrong. That's three days and three hours from now, exactly. Maybe we can get them to leave at six oh three, and that'll give us three days, three hours, and three minutes."

"Wow," Dini says. "I wish I could figure out stuff like that."

Mom sticks her head through the doorway. "How are you two?"

"We're fine," says Maddie.

"Just fine," says Dini.

Dad peeks in. "How are the Velcro girls doing?"

"Fine," they say. "Just fine."

Maddie's mom calls to ask about them too. Everyone is suddenly terribly interested in Maddie and Dini. Don't they have anything else to do?

Dini shuts the door to her room. Maddie hums a song from MJTJ. "Got to get that CD," she says.

Then they pull out the rainbow-colored sari that Dini begged Mom to give her from her sari collection. It looks a bit like the one Dolly has on when she's getting her big award for bravery at the end of the movie. Well, maybe not quite enough green, and certainly not enough silver, but sometimes you just make do.

Dini and Maddie grab opposite ends of the sari and dance around the room together while belting out what they can remember of "Sunno-sunno" until they collapse in a heap, exhausted.

The day arrives. That day.

"Please can we leave at six oh three?" Dini begs. "Please, please, please? Promise me you won't pull out of the driveway until six oh three?"

Mom looks about to say something and then does not.

"Six-zero-three," Dad promises.

And so the hours and minutes tick down the way hours and minutes do, and it is sixteen minutes to six. The suitcases are loaded in the taxi. Passports and itineraries have been checked and double-checked.

Hugs have been hugged. Sad but true, a few tears have also been shed, because how is it humanly possible to say good-bye without them?

"Wait a minute!" Dini is about to get into the car when she remembers something. "Did anyone check the mail today?"

"Not me," Dad says. "Did you?"

Mom shakes her head. Dad says something about address changes and the tenants sending on mail, but Dini is already running to the mailbox.

In it is a single envelope. Cream colored, with

little embossed flowers on it. "Dini Kumaran," it says. Dolly has replied to Dini.

Dini screams and runs back waving the envelope. She hugs Maddie. Maddie hugs her back. Dini opens the letter.

June 9, 2010

Dearest Friend and Fan:

I am always so happy to hear from you. Thank you for your kind letters. Please keep them coming.

I know you will understand that I receive many letters from all over the world, and so I cannot reply to each of your questions personally, even though I take every single one most seriously.

You are my hope. You are my delight. You know the rest.

Best wishes,

Dolly Singh

And now it is 6:03, and Dad, true to his promise, tells the cabdriver it is time to leave. Maddie waves, and dabs her eyes. Dini waves. Her lip quivers, but she makes it straighten up.

The cab backs out of the driveway. Before Dini can untangle the mess of sadness and excitement and oh-no-now-what coursing through her, they are on I-95, headed north to that big airport in Baltimore, from which so many people leave when they have to go overseas.

Dini reads the letter over and over. It is a sign, small but sure. The "Dearest Friend and Fan" part feels good. So do the "hope" and "delight" lines. An ignorant reader would not get the reference, of course, but Dini does indeed know the rest of that song.

She hums it now, hums that hope and delight song all the way to the airport. It is the only way she knows not to cry.

Chapter Ten

Swapnagiri

"HEY THERE," SAYS DAD AS THEY drive from the airport in a white Qualis, which is what Toyota calls this kind of a van in India, "are you okay? Right as rain back there?"

Mom says nothing, but that is because her right ear got stopped up somewhere between Baltimore and Frankfurt and hasn't popped yet, so she can't hear very well.

Dini groans. Right as rain she is not. The backseat of the Qualis is way too cluttered for comfort, and she has lost one of her sandals under a bag, which is most annoying. Dolly's letter is in her carry-on bag, and she can't even get at it to read it once more. She would like to do that because in addition to making her very tired and sleepy, all this travel has made her a bit . . . worried. That maybe in the excitement of getting that letter, she didn't read it properly. When she looked at it last on the plane, before getting off at this airport-that-was-not-Bombay, it looked as if the signature was just a printed one.

"Dearest Friend and Fan" . . . could it be? Is it possible that what she got back was only a form letter?

Dini's thoughts are dizzying, or maybe it is just that the driver of the van, a man named Veeran with a fiercely-pointed mustache, is driving rather fast. Every time he honks the horn, which is every few minutes—*bebeep-bebeep!*—Dini's parents clutch their seats and beg him to slow down.

"Don't worry," Veeran says. "You are in the hands of a superfine driver and mechanic."

It is entirely unreasonable to expect a normal person to sit in a plane for fifteen hours at a time without getting fidgety, and then to plunk that same person into a van for still more sitting. Every time Dini visits India with Mom and Dad, she keeps expecting they will make the planes faster, but they are still not fast enough. Now she is getting cross-eyed trying to figure out what time it is in Maryland and when would be a good time to try to call Maddie.

But then Dini sees something that knocks all these things out of her mind.

She sees something green and silver on a billboard.

And she sees a face. What a face. Dini has been looking for Dolly posters ever since they left the airport. She knew she would see one sooner or later. How could she not? Everyone in India loves Dolly.

She can't stop herself from crying out, "Slow down, slow down!"

Veeran slams on the brakes, and the Qualis screeches to a crawl in the middle of the road, making all the cars and trucks and scooters in back of it burst into a cacophony of honking.

Mom wrings her hands in a panicky gesture that Dini notes, even in her dazed state. It's practically fillum-worthy.

Dad says, "Hey! What happened?"

But Veeran the driver is shaking his head from side to side, which is what people do here when they mean to tell you that they are with you. He says, "You *know* our superfine, tip-top film star Dolly Singh?"

"Yes," Dini says. No one knows Dolly Singh's

superfine tip-topness like she does. Well, Maddie does, but she is on the other side of the world right now.

Veeran picks up speed again, honking his horn to get three bicyclists and a donkey out of the way of the Qualis. "There is one more Dolly Singh picture," he says, turning around to point it out.

Dad clutches the dashboard for comfort. Mom clutches her head.

Then Veeran the driver says something that makes Dini shriek in astonishment. He says, "Miss Dolly Singh is now in Swapnagiri."

Dini says, "In *Swap*nagiri?"

"Nandu," says Dad, as if Dini is the one who is making him nervous.

The white van is heading out of the city now and into countryside with rice fields and big spreading trees.

Wow-wow-wow! Can this be true? Dini thought she was going to be miles and miles away from Bombay, the center of the filmi universe, and now it seems that Dolly has come to the very place they're headed for! She's come to Dini. It seems too good to be true.

"Are you *sure*?" she says to Veeran.

He shakes his head from side to side to side, very very fast, he is that sure.

He weaves between two rows of buses.

"Quite sure," he says, slamming the gas pedal to the floor, so that the Qualis engine revs into a victorious roar. "It's a small town. People talk. Normally I don't pay attention, but my missus and me, we love Dolly Singh's movies."

"Do you know where she lives?" Dini says.

"Oh my, no," says Veeran. "I'm sure she does not want everyone and their brother-in-law turning up on her doorstep."

"I'd love to meet her," Dini says. "I've seen every single one of her fillums."

"My missus and me also," says Veeran.

"Me and my friend Maddie," says Dini, "we're both Dolly fans."

"Really?" says Veeran, taking both hands off the steering wheel to show his amazement at what a small world it is. Mom and Dad clutch at each other now.

"So it's true, Miss Nandini," Veeran says, "that they like our Dolly Singh in America also."

Dini tells him about how she and Maddie would have gone to Bollywood dance camp together this summer, only she is here now.

"My little girl is too small now to take dance classes," Veeran says, "but she likes Dolly Singh's songs also. Every time they play on the radio, she laughs loudly."

Life is an astonishing thing. Who would have guessed that the driver of this van, sent by the clinic to meet Mom and Dad and Dini at the airport and bring them to Swapnagiri, would turn out to be a true fan? Who would have guessed that he would bring Dini this glad news that seems almost too good to be true?

Veeran picks up speed. Dad suggests Dini should let him drive and not distract him with her chatter. They are now on some very twisty bends of a mountain road. There are signs: SLOW DOWN and TOO FAST? WHY TEMPT FATE? And this one, which seems like good advice: ARRIVE ALIVE.

Dad is now saying something to Mom about the rupee-dollar exchange getting more favorable, which sounds like complete gibberish, and if he thinks that's not distracting to the driver of the van, then Dini thinks he should think again. Especially as he has to talk extra loud on account of Mom's stuffed-up ear.

Dini's own thoughts are twisting and tumbling so fast in her head that they are making her dizzy. She's got so much to do.

She has to find Dolly now. She can't be this close to her and not meet her in person.

She'll tell her, "I was born—born!—on the same day that your very first movie was released."

And Dolly will say, as she says in MJTJ, "Kismat ki baat hai." Which it is, of course. It is just a matter of kismet, which some people think of as fate, but it's so much more. It is about things that were just meant to be, like Dolly being in Swapnagiri when all the common sense in the world might suggest she'd be in Bombay, the center of the filmi universe.

As soon as they are unpacked and settled in, Dini will invite Dolly to come visit her.

Dolly will come. Dolly will invite Dini to be part of her next movie project. A scriptwriter, perhaps, or that person who is rather peculiarly called a grip. Dini's name will be on the credits. . . .

At this point Dini realizes that in that letter

she wrote to Dolly, she made a silly mistake. She should have sent Dolly her address in Swapnagiri. How on Earth can she expect Dolly to come visit her without knowing where she'll be?

"Sunno-sunno," she hums to herself, "dekho-dekho." That helps to calm her down, as it always does.

Swapnagiri is not as big as Bombay. It is probably not even as big as Takoma Park, Maryland. Dini will just have to listen-listen and look-look, and she will find Dolly.

Chapter Eleven

Sunny Villa, Take One

"SIR, SWAPNAGIRI MARKET," says Veeran to Dini's father, waving his hand at houses and shops as if he is introducing the Taj Mahal. The market whizzes past. Veeran leans on his horn, scattering people, goats, and chickens.

Dini listen-listens. She look-looks. This is a busy kind of place. Dolly is nowhere to be seen in it. This is going to be more difficult than Dini thought.

The houses lean comfortably into one another, with shops on the ground floor and washing strung on lines along their rooftops like bright flags. Dini can see kids playing with marbles on the sidewalk. She can see people selling oranges and pineapples. A woman pushes a cart piled high with ripe, yellow bananas so tiny that Dini could probably eat half a dozen just for a snack.

But of Dolly there is no sign.

Veeran points out a temple, a church, and a mosque. He shows them the post office. In her mind Dini can see a vision of Dolly buying a string of jasmine flowers to put in her hair, or leading some kind of procession, or collecting funds on behalf of orphaned children. Every single one of those places could be a Dolly backdrop, even the post office. Maybe especially the post office, with its red mailbox that looks like an oversize fire hydrant. Dolly could dance around that, all twinkling toes and *chan-chan-chan* ankle bells. But in reality, sad to say, Dolly is not actually doing any of this at this moment.

The van turns onto a red dirt road and jerks to a stop outside a gate. Dad lowers the window and says something. At first Dini thinks her father is talking to himself. Then she sees that he's talking to a man sitting by the road, chewing on a bit of grass.

It turns out the man's name is Sampy, which sounds like a happy kind of name, only he isn't. He should have been named Grumpy. It seems that no one has told him Dini's family is arriving, and he likes to be able to plan his day.

"Is this it?" Dini asks. "Are we there?"

Mom beams at her. Oh, right. She can't hear.

On both sides of the van are fields full of green bushes, with houses scattered about between them. "Tea-gardens," Veeran says. "Houses are rented out, but Sunny Villa Estates is still a working tea-garden. Mr. Chickoo Dev, of Dev Tea, is the owner." Dini can only think, What a great place for a movie shoot!

Sampy takes a key off a giant key ring and gives it gloomily to Dad. Then the van is bumping along once more. Dini looks back over the pile of luggage to see Sampy closing the gate and going back to sitting on the side of the road, chewing on his bit of grass.

The van stops in front of a brick-red house. Veeran gets down to open the gate.

"Another gate?" says Dini.

"That one was just the starting gate," Dad says.

"What?" says Dini, digging her missing sandal out from under a bag on the floor of the van.

"Joke," says Dad. "Like a starting gate at a race-track?"

"This isn't a racetrack," Dini points out, putting on the sandal.

"A movie clapboard, then," Dad says. "You know, those black and white things they clank together when they say—"

"Take one!" Dini cries. At last Dad has found nifty words that make sense. "I didn't know that's what they were called."

"Yes indeed. Clapboard," says Dad happily.

This is it. Take one.

"Welcome to Sunny Villa Estates, cottage number six," says Dad.

Dini opens the door of the van and steps out. The moment her feet touch the sloping concrete driveway, a wave of sleep hits her. Jet lag—she forgot how awful it is. She stands there, swaying a little. To her dazed eyes it seems the house is moving too, in a slightly nauseating way. She expects tree branches to move in this manner, but not a house.

Dini clutches at her nice green and silver scarf that she is wearing for good luck. The house steadies itself. Its little upstairs windows with funny-looking shutters give it a blinky look.

Veeran and Dad unload the baggage. While they get the door open, Dini sits down on the front step and puts her head in her hands because it suddenly feels heavy, as if her neck will no longer support it.

Mom folds some rupee notes into Veeran's hand, and he nods his thanks and gets back into the Qualis. He'll be here the next day, he says, to take Mom to the clinic. She protests, but he will have none of it. He intends to transport her here and there and back again, at least until she gets used to the way things work in Swapnagiri. "It is my job," he insists, and seems to take it seriously.

"Mom," Dini says, "do you think I could get to meet her?"

Mom looks up. She rubs her stuffy ear and breathes deeply, as if hoping that will fix it. She says, "I know. I can't believe it either."

"Dolly," Dini says, forming the words very clearly and slowly on the off chance that Mom has begun to read lips. "You think she's really here?"

"Who would have thought it?" says Mom. "Pure good luck. The best kind of coincidence."

"That's just it," Dini says. "We're here, and so is Dolly."

Mom smiles at her the way that grown-ups do when they think their kid, whom they raised and love, is cute, but they are really thinking about something else. "Daddy had trouble finding a house at first," Mom explains. "And this one just happened to become available for rent."

Oh. She's talking about the house.

Soon Mom is on the cell phone calling the clinic. "Hello? Yes, it's Dr. Kumaran. We just got here. . . . I'm sorry, my ear is all blocked up, what did you say?"

Dini leaves her to it.

Dad is sharing quiet time with his laptop. Dini asks him, "Daddy, do you think it's coincidence that we're here and Dolly's here too?"

Dad looks up. "Ah, an existential question," he says happily. He rubs his hands, which usually means he is going to say something very long that may or may not make much sense. "It depends, I think, on how you look at it." He adds some rambling comments about randomness and patterns and mathematical probability, and some other things he seems to care deeply about.

"Is all that for real?" she says.

"Is bubble gum pink?" says Dad cheerfully. "Does your teddy bear have ears?"

"Bubble gum's not *always* pink," Dini points out reasonably, "and it's a bunny, not a bear." Her parents sometimes forget she's not in kindergarten any more. Maddie has that exact same problem with her mom. Being a kid in a grown-up world is, as Dad might say, no bowl of mangoes.

Maddie. "Can I call Maddie?" Dini says. She likes the thought of coincidence being more than just random chance. It sounds promising, the kind of thing that turns script potential into script only (as they say in the filmi world). She thinks, This is all like a script, and I could make it work that way. Maddie and me, we could work together to make this movie happen. The Dini Meets Dolly movie, sometimes also known as the Life Becomes Perfect When You Work at It movie. A creative project, that's what filmi people would call this.

So what if Swapnagiri is far from Takoma Park? There's the phone and e-mail and . . .

Dad looks at his watch. "It's now three a.m. in Maryland," he says. "I don't think Maddie's mother will appreciate a phone call at this time."

In filmi terms, Dini can see there are all kinds of problems when you are directing a creative project with someone and your codirector is halfway around the world from you. She pulls out her stripy green notebook and quickly writes: "Coincidence." She adds a question mark. She likes the look of it and adds two more.

Now that she is here in this Dream Mountain place, Dini can see that it is up to her to listen-listen, look-look, and find Dolly Singh—which she will, she is sure of it, just as soon as she

can stop falling

asleep.

She is in a white van that is driving backward really fast, and she is yelling at the driver to stop-stop-stop because there is someone there, dancing through rows and rows of tea bushes and she has to find out who it is.

It is. Of course it is. It is Dolly in a new movie, newer even than MJTJ.

It's just before the close-up, one in which Dolly's face is all dreamy-beautiful and floaty and she's wearing those sparkly silver earrings. If only this crazy driver would stop, Dini could get out and see. It's a test, she figures. If she can just move quickly enough, she'll get there.

She'll go up to Dolly, who's stamping her feet and snapping her fingers, with the bangles on her arms going chan-chan-chan. She'll catch up with her. Dolly will turn in surprise and look right at Dini, her superdevoted fan.

Dini will say—

"Stop!" Dini yells. "Stop!" She opens her eyes to a thunderous knocking. Someone is hammering on the front door.

Chapter Twelve

Sorry to Inform

COOLED BY THE SHADE of a spreading tree just outside the grounds of the Blue Mountain School (a very fine school indeed—a school to which everyone coming to Swapnagiri wishes to send their children), a man stretches out peacefully under a clear blue sky.

The man is a goatherd. Naturally, his goats mill around him, cropping the grass.

Nearby a low, broad-leafed plant is putting out purple buds. This is no ordinary plant. It is the kurinji plant, and the goatherd knows that it is a sign of great good luck. This beautiful purply blue flower, for which these mountains are named, blooms only once every twelve years.

The goatherd is just beginning to daydream about the good luck that this flowering will bring him. A little money, perhaps—why not?—will come to him as a result of this good luck. Maybe he can move up from goats to a cow or two. Then he can sell the milk and buy some chickens. Their eggs will no doubt be appreciated by that nice Mr. Mani who runs a very fine bakery on Blue Mountain Road. Those fresh eggs will make Mr. Mani's cakes even richer and finer than they are now. The goatherd sighs in delight at the thought that the eggs from his yet-to-be-bought chickens are giving so much happiness.

With the money from the sale of the eggs—

A most distressing sound interrupts this lovely stream of thought. It makes the goatherd sit bolt upright and wonder in dismay if his dream has turned into a nightmare.

There it comes again.

And again.

It is an unmistakable sound. It is the sound of someone screaming.

The goatherd leaps up, grabs his cloth bundle, and glances around him fearfully. Who could that be?

The Blue Mountain School is closed for the summer, so who could possibly be lurking in one of those many buildings on the school grounds? And not just lurking peacefully and quietly, but screaming.

Is it a ghost? Kurinji flower or no kurinji flower, the goatherd is taking no chances. He hurries his precious animals off to find a better grazing spot.

Who can blame him? Any sensible person hearing that scream would want to get as far away from it as possible. It was that kind of scream.

Screams of this nature are best heard in a movie theater, when the heroine of a three-hour filmi epic has just reached the point of deep distress. In a movie theater, the audience understands. They even sympathize. They may find themselves getting misty-eyed, waiting for the story to turn and sprint to a hopeful scene, an easing of tension, a resolution of the crisis. In fact, they have almost certainly plunked down their handfuls of rupees in order to see the story proceed at a hurtling gallop toward its joyful finish.

But a scream, just by itself, with no story to match—what is the use of that?

Life, however, is so often not what it seems. The goatherd does not know this, but that scream does have a story to go with it. Quite a story, in fact.

The person whose screams have just demonstrated the most excellent capacity of her lungs has just received a letter. She has read it from salutation to signature. In fact, she has read it three times, in her room in the Blue Mountain School guesthouse.

The person in question is in that room because she has been offered temporary refuge and haven there by her good friend Meena, who admires her greatly and who also happens to be the principal of this fine school.

The screamer reads the letter over and over. But no matter how often she casts her desperate eyes over it, it still says the same thing.

June 13, 2010

Dear Ms. Singh,

We are very sorry to inform you that Starlite Studios will not be renewing your contract with us, due to a certain falling-out that you have had with our major sponsor and most generous patron, the respected

Mr. Chickoo Dev, of Dev Tea
(Private) Limited, who was going
to permit us to film on his
estate without charge simply
as a big favor to you. We think
you know the falling-out to
which we refer.

Now, of course, he has changed
his mind. So we must likewise
advise you that we are changing
ours. You may consider that
this project has been, as we say
in the business, indefinitely
shelved.

Yours truly,

S. Dustup

President and CEO
Starlite Studios

P.S. You called him a potato
nose.

Chapter Thirteen

Read Between the Smudges

June 17, 2010

Meena darling,

I am sending this by Speed Post so it gets to you before you leave. Sampy stops by every now and then, very kindly, to make sure I am comfortable, so I'll ask him to post it for me.

I know you told me I could stay here while you were in Australia and I was visiting a certain person in this town who shall remain nameless. Visiting him with great hopes for happiness, no less. But I'm writing to ask you if I can stay longer.

How long? I don't know. How long does it take to mend a broken heart?

I am distraught. And devastated.

It all began with an argument. Go to the city because of a noise in the car? Or stay home and listen to music and watch a beautiful restored copy of that lovely old movie *Shree 420* that I got with my own two hands straight from the studio office in Bombay? With that song in it that is iconic. I tell you, simply iconic. "Mera Joota hai Japani" . . . that one. Brings tears to my eyes just thinking of it, makes me proud to be Indian, I tell you.

I know, I know, it seems like a small thing, but it was just the beginning.

At any rate there is now no more engagement. I threw the ring out of the car. No use groaning. It's done. I tell you, it felt good. I listened to see if it hit a rock or not but that stupid car was making such a racket it could have shattered a window of some house down the hill and I wouldn't have heard a thing.

I hope it fell into a pile of cow dung. No. I
don't. I have been crying ever since. Now look.
I've cried all over this letter. And I'm too
tired to write it again. so you will have to read
between the smudges.

The thing is. I can't stand the thought of going
back to Bombay. Because—mirchi on a wound.
I tell you—Soli's pulling out of the project. So
not only my happiness is gone but my career also.

Hugs and kisses to you and your children and
grandchildren. Did they really get to see my
movies in Australia? What a thrill. I am so
blessed to have such a good friend as you.

Love.

Dolly

Chapter Fourteen

Swapnagiri Post Office

"SPEED POST TO AUSTRALIA?" says Ramanna the postal carrier in astonishment. "I have never heard of such a thing."

"It is possible," says the Swapnagiri postmaster, pushing his glasses up his nose and squinting at the letter that has just been presented to him by a man with a single beetling eyebrow. "Yes, I think I know how to process that. Let me see. . . ." He pulls his fat green regulations notebook off the shelf. "Yes, there it is. Item number fifty-six under instruction number 375 b (i) c."

The man pays and leaves, entrusting the letter to the care of the Swapnagiri postmaster.

"So much money?" says Ramanna, picking up the envelope and tallying up the cost of the stamps. "It costs that many hundreds of rupees to send Speed Post items to foreign countries? Waste, waste."

"It's their wish, if they want to pay," the postmaster points out.

A mild rebuke, but Ramanna is too busy fuming at the thought. "How will it get there?" he demands.

"There is such a thing as a plane," the postmaster reminds him.

"Terrible, loud things," says Ramanna. He watches while the postmaster shows him the correct forms to complete so that the fat letter with the curiously smudgy handwritten address can be sent to Australia superfast, so it can travel thousands of miles and over the ocean, and yet arrive in just a couple of days.

He remains unconvinced. "Where is the need for so much hurry-burry, I say?" says Ramanna.

Chapter Fifteen

Monkeys

DINI SEEMS TO HAVE SLEPT for half a day and a whole night, because it is now morning. Mom has gone to the clinic already.

"But it's Saturday," Dini says, rolling herself out of bed.

"Not yet," Dad says. "It's Friday. And anyway, Saturday's a working day here."

"I thought moving to India was supposed to be fun," Dini says. This is no fun at all.

The someone who hammered on the front door and woke Dini up was Sampy the watchman. He brought candles, and Dad is now putting one in every room in the house.

"Why candles?" Dini asks.

"In case the electricity goes off," says Dad.

"Will it?" Dini turns the faucet on.

Dad waves his arms around in a who-knows kind

of way and plunks a candle down on the desk in Dini's room.

But the electricity is not the thing that has gone. The faucet squawks at Dini. "Hey, what happened to the water?" she says.

"We had to shut it off," Dad says. "I'm going up on the roof to see what's up."

"Why?" Dini says, but he's gone already. People are zipping in and out of scenes like clueless extras instead of the major actors they are.

Forget showering and brushing teeth. Dini changes quickly. She tucks her green notebook and pen into the pocket of her jeans and goes down to the kitchen. She peels herself one of those tiny bananas just like the ones she saw on that cart when they drove through the market. She eats it. She is not going to be zipping around. She has things to think about.

She is just peeling another banana when thumping and shouting noises break out on the roof. With a sigh, Dini takes a bite of the tiny fruit—the whole thing is only two bites—and goes out to see what is happening. She climbs the ladder that goes up the side of the house, leading to the rooftop. Dad is up

there waving his arms. "What are you doing?" Dini says.

He half turns. "Aaaah!" he shouts, and now he is waving at her.

"What?" Dini says, clambering up, still holding that banana.

"Look out!" shouts Dad.

Just then something comes barreling across the roof. Dini screams. The something grabs at Dini's banana with scrabbly little hands. It bares its teeth. Then it sits down and eats the remaining bite of the fruit, skin and all.

"Monkeys," Dad says in disgust. "They've made a big mess in the water-tank."

"Open the vent, sir!" shouts a voice from down below. "Pull the levers down, sir. No, no, sir, push them up." Sampy the grumpy watchman has come to help.

Dad mutters something under his breath.

"Better boil all the water from now on, sir," says Sampy, still being helpful. "The water supply, sir, is very fine, normally—springwater in our hills is world famous—but if there are drowned monkeys . . ." He purses his lips and shrugs his shoulders to explain the hopelessness of it. It seems to please him in a gloomy kind of way.

"You really think . . . ?" Dad pushes a vent open and quickly peers inside. "No, thank goodness," he says, "only a lot of half-eaten flowers."

"Something has disturbed those monkeys, is it?" says Sampy, glowering at Dad as if it's his fault the monkeys are upset.

"It would seem so," says Dad.

Sampy moves into interview mode. "How is it with American monkeys, sir? They are prone to being high-strung like our Blue Mountain monkeys? Or maybe they are more placid because of the colder climate?"

Dad has to admit there are no monkeys in America, at least not in the wild like this.

"No monkeys?" says Sampy. He gives Dad a pitying look, as if he cannot imagine how people can live in such a place, with no monkeys to liven up their days.

Dini says, shuffling along the sloping red-tiled roof, "I wish we'd had monkeys in Maryland. That would have been fun." She climbs onto the platform at one end, where the water-tank sits, and peers inside. "How'd they get in?"

"Perhaps we can make some arrangement to send some monkeys to the U.S.," Sampy says. "To add a little bit of action to the American landscape."

"The lid," Dad says sadly. "Someone must have left it open." He shakes his head at Sampy, but Sampy is too busy with his export plans to notice.

Broken branches are floating on the water in the tank, along with half-eaten stalks of flowers that the monkeys seem to have ripped out of the garden. "Where did they go?" Dini says.

"Vanished," says Sampy dolefully. "Wreaking havoc, no doubt, on the next mountaintop."

Monkeys on the roof! This is something to tell Maddie about. Dini does not remember a single Dolly movie in which monkeys mess up a person's roof. But it would work, she thinks. What a scene it would make. They could even have a dance number with Dolly and the monkeys fighting off a villain or something. She should tell Dolly, when she finds her.

"You are not needing me now, sir?" says Sampy the watchman in a hopeful sort of way.

Dad says that, on the contrary, he will certainly

need Sampy's help to get the branches out of the tank.

"Delighted, sir," says Sampy in a voice loaded with gloom.

"This is going to take a while," Dini's father says, matching Sampy's frown.

"That's okay," Dini says, trying to make things better. "I'm just taking notes."

Dad seems surprised. "Notes? For what?"

"A movie," Dini says. She settles herself down on the narrow, flat ledge and leans against the water-tank. She pulls out her notebook. She tests the green pen, and it still glitters as well as it did when Maddie first gave it to her. Was that a week ago? Ten days? Nine? It feels like forever. She writes a few quick notes for possible story lines.

One involves monkeys on a rooftop.

Another involves Dolly getting caught in a rain-storm. Dini comes by and sees her. She has twisted her ankle walking in the rain. Sampy comes by and . . . no, that won't work because how can you connect things that do not seem to have any way of being connected? This plot-fixing business is tough.

Dad wipes his face on his sleeve. "Nandu, *rani* . . ."

"Yes?"

Dad says, "There really isn't room for three of us on the roof, so do you think . . . ?"

"Can I go out there, then?" Dini says, waving the green pen at the great wide expanse of Sunny Villa Estates, that strange mix of deeply tracked red dirt roads and green, green tea-gardens.

"Sure," Dad says. "Just don't go too far."

Dini is off the roof in a quick movie minute. Something about this place makes her want to run down the lane and through those tea-gardens, smelling the smoke that trails up the hillsides from cooking fires below, all of it mixed up with slightly rotting leaves and a kind of misty dampness.

People think India is all hot and dusty. But here is Swapnagiri and it is singing out to Dini to come take a look at it. It looks so much like the setting of a Dolly movie that it makes her heart turn over.

"Stay inside the main gate," Dad calls after her.

"Okaaaaaaay!" Dini calls back, and she is already running.

Chapter Sixteen

Priya

DINI IS THUDDING down the road the way the monkeys thudded over the rooftop. She misses her bike, which she would be riding in Maryland, and Maddie would be riding hers, so really what she misses is Maddie.

If Maddie were here, she would be helping Dini to look for Dolly. But then Dini thinks, Well, this is the thing I am supposed to do here in Swapnagiri— find Dolly Singh. That is my job.

She repeats this thought to herself as she slows down.

This is why I'm here.

This is why I'm . . .

This is why . . .

This is . . .

Why . . .

She walks along the red dirt road and repeats it

some more. *Why I am . . . in India . . . this is why. . . .* The words keep time nicely with her slowing-down feet. They make her feel slightly heroic.

A crowd of women and girls come up the road, with enormous bundles of sticks balanced on their heads. They look at Dini but they don't stop. Nor does the man with a herd of goats who *click-click-clicks* at his animals and keeps them running right past Dini's legs. They leave behind a goaty smell and a little pile of poopy pellets that she just misses stepping into.

She keeps on going for a while. Then she stops to take a breath under a tree with red flowers hanging from it like bottlebrushes.

"Hello," says the tree.

Dini jumps and almost drops her green stripy notebook in the dirt. She grabs at it just in time. A girl with a perfectly square haircut is peering down at her through the lacy green leaves.

"Sorry," says the girl. She shapes her mouth into a round O and makes a sound just like one of the little birds that are buzzing around the red bottle-brush flowers. Dini has never heard anyone do such a good imitation of a small, buzzy bird.

The girl jumps down and lands with a thump. She brushes feathery little red petals out of her hair. She looks at Dini's astonished face and starts to laugh. She laughs so hard she has to hold her side.

"What's so funny?" Dini says, annoyed. Why is the girl laughing at her?

The girl finally quits laughing and introduces herself. "I'm Priya."

"I'm Dini. You always make bird noises?" Dini says.

"Not only birds. Listen." She closes her eyes, and she makes a whole lot of noises one after the other—a car horn; a long, tinny whistle; the moo of a cow; and something that sounds like gushing water. And here is the thing: She does them all equally well.

"Wow," Dini says.

"From America—I can Tell from your Accent." Dini notices something else. Some of the things Priya says are meant to be in capital letters. "Where?"

"Takoma Park, Maryland," Dini tells her.

"My parents are in Washington, D.C." Priya says. "Right Now."

"Really? Washington, D.C.! We're opposites." Dini means Priya's parents going from India to America and hers doing the opposite. She shows Priya her boarding pass that she has stuck into the back page of her notebook. Priya regards it seriously.

"We Are Opposites," Priya says. She knows exactly what Dini means, which is a thing Dini's used to with Maddie but really doesn't expect from total strangers.

"Are you going to stay Here for a while?" Priya wants to know.

"Two years," Dini says. She will be thirteen before they leave, which seems an impossible-to-reach goal. "You?"

"I think a year," Priya says. "They're in Washington now, but Afterwards they're going to Chile for five months and then to Haiti, so I'm staying Here. With my Uncle."

"Oh." And here Dini has been thinking only her parents would do a crazy thing like pick up and move halfway across the world.

"I Miss Bombay," Priya says.

"Bom*bay!*" Dini yells, forgetting all about parents and jobs and travel.

"Yo." Priya rubs her ear. "Don't Shout."

"Sorry." But Dini has to tell her. About Maddie and the whole idea of coincidences that are more than random—although she is not sure she completely gets the details of that—and of course Dolly.

"So now I heard she's here!" Dini says at last, finishing up the story of her parents and the move and Maddie's idea and the letter to Dolly and oh yes, the reply, the reply! "Do you know where she is? I have to find her."

Priya narrows her eyes until they're all slitty. Then she shakes her head. "No," she says, but she says it as if she had to think first.

"She's not here? Or you don't know?"

But Priya seems to be busy looking into the distance and making that crazy bird-cheep noise that Dini wishes she could make, but now she wants Priya to quit it, just quit it and talk instead.

"Talking is good," she wants to say. "There is nothing wrong with talking." She wants Priya to tell her whatever it is she's not telling her about Dolly.

And then when Priya does talk, Dini almost wishes she hadn't, because this is what Priya says:

"Dolly Singh, Dolly Singh, I'm sick as mud of Dolly Singh. Turn on the TV, it's Dolly. Talk to the neighbor, it's Dolly. You'd think no one has anything better to talk about than Dolly, Dolly, Dolly."

"Excuuuuse me," says Dini, affronted. "You don't understand. It's a matter of . . ." She has to stop to think what exactly it is a matter of. "I have to make sure she's okay," she ends lamely.

Priya bursts out laughing. "She's Okay," she says when she's finished cracking up. "Oh, I can Assure you that She is Okay."

Dini wants to ask how she knows and does she know Dolly and a dozen other questions. But just then a bright yellow car drives toward them. It slows down, stops. A man leans out of the driver's window. Dini thinks, He has the kind of face where you only remember the nose, not to be mean or anything.

The man says, all out of breath, "Priya! There you are. I've been looking for you all over."

Priya says, "I have to Go. See you later." Was there an uppercase in that seeing Dini later? Dini can't tell. She waves and says, "See you Later," trying it out loud in that Priya way, "Later" with a capital *L* leading the word along.

But Priya's gone in the car already, and Dini finds that she is instead talking to some tea pickers who have arrived to take a break in the shade of the tree with red flowers. They do not look as if they get what she's saying, capital letters or not. They are looking as if this is their space and Dini is in the way.

Dini walks slowly along the red dirt road back toward cottage number 6, and she starts to wonder. Does Priya know Dolly Singh or not? And who is the man in the yellow car?

She passes a weedy garden. The woman who is digging in the garden straightens up. A small, yappy sausage dog rolls in the dirt at her feet. The woman looks at her watch.

"Can you tell me what time it is?" Dini says.

"Two," the woman says in a whispery voice. "Time to give this messy doggy a bath." And she scoops up the dog and heads inside.

Which makes Dini wonder what time it is in Maryland right now this minute. It's two in the afternoon here, and the sun is bright and beamy, quite unlike how Dini is feeling. She counts the hours backward the way you have to do, and it's nine and a half hours' difference. That means it's early in the morning. Maddie won't mind.

When Dini gets back to cottage number 6, Dad and Sampy are deep in conversation about the cost of washers and gaskets and stuff, as some of the faucets (they call them taps here) seem to be drippy.

"Dad," says Dini, "can I call Maddie?"

"Sure," Dad says, although Dini doesn't think he really heard her. She could probably have said, "Can I pack my suitcase and go back to Maryland?" and he would have said "Sure" to that, too.

She goes inside the house and picks up Dad's cell phone and hits the long, long, long series of numbers you have to hit to call Takoma Park, Maryland, all the way from India.

The phone rings. Maddie's mom answers it. It is four thirty in the morning. Dini got the time all wrong. Maddie's mom says, "Can you call back later?" Then she says, "Oh, wait. Maddie's up. Here she is."

"Hi, Maddie," Dini says. "Sorry to wake you up."

"What time is it?" Maddie sounds half asleep.

"Four thirty. For you. It's two in the afternoon here. Sorry, Maddie, but I think I found someone who knows something, only she's not telling."

"What do you mean?" Maddie sounds confused. "Who? Knows something about what?"

"About Dolly!" Dini says. "She's here. In Swapnagiri."

"Wow. No kidding? Really?" Now Maddie sounds wide awake. "Oh, Dini, that is so wowza-yowza-exciting. I just know you'll find her, you will, you will, you will. Oh, Dini . . ."

Dini starts to tell Maddie it may not be that simple, but then she realizes that it would take way too long to tell Maddie about Priya, and how do you explain a girl who makes bird-cheeps, anyway, and falls out of trees on people? Dini could try the bird-cheeps, but she does not know if that will help. Then there are all the questions. What does

Priya know? What is she not telling, and why?

It's all too complicated for a phone call, especially when Maddie is now going on about how clever Dini is, and then she goes on to something else, something long and convoluted about dreams coming true.

An e-mail. Dini decides she'll have to tell Maddie about Priya in an e-mail. She'd better tell her it's not going that smoothly so far, even if Dolly is here. That itself seems such an impossible thing that Dini wonders, Was Veeran even right about that? Did he make a mistake? Or worse. Much worse. Did Dini imagine it all? She was pretty tired and jet-lagged at the time.

Dini tries to herd all these thoughts into words that will make sense, but Maddie is still talking. "Don't forget to get her autograph for me, okay?"

Dini has heard of hearts sinking. She has always thought it was an odd thing for a heart to do.

But now she thinks she knows what that means.

"You promised," Maddie says.

"Okay," says Dini. "I mean yes, Maddie. Yes."

And she hangs up, but only after Maddie has blown kisses to her over the phone and told her to remember that half those kisses were for Dolly, and Dini should be sure to pass them on.

Definitely, at this very moment, Dini's heart is doing that sinking thing.

Chapter Seventeen

Gloom

From: dini@swpn.com.in
To: hurraymaddie@globenet.link
Subject: Dolly
Date: Friday, June 18, 2010, 20:09:33 IST

Maddie I tried to tell you but it's not so easy. I met
this girl called Priya. At first I thought she was
going to be my friend but now I'm not so sure. I
think she knows something about Dolly, but she's
not telling.

Not even half an hour after Dini has sent that
e-mail zinging into cyberspace, the phone rings.
"For you," says Dad.

It's Maddie. She says, "I just got your e-mail. So
who's this friend again?" Under the question is a
little wobble in the voice.

"Well, no," says Dini, and she's really answering another unspoken question. "She isn't exactly. I mean, I thought maybe she could be, but she's not . . . not really."

"I don't know, Dini," says Maddie. "I mean, I'm not telling you about all the new friends I'm making."

"You are?" says Dini. "You're making new friends?"

"Well, no," says Maddie. The word trails off into a little upswing, trails away into the distance between them. Nooooo . . .

Dini is about to set it all straight, as much as she can, even in her own mind. She wants to explain further about Veeran and how he is a fan and an ally, and how Priya knows Dolly all right but she is certainly hiding something, so does that make her an antagonist or what?

But right then she notices that Mom and Dad are just around the corner in the kitchen, talking to each other.

If Dini can hear them talking about where the spoons should go, they can probably also hear what she's saying to Maddie. Would they listen?

Sure they would. Parents are nosy people.

Dini does not know how Mom and Dad will react to her Dolly-finding efforts, but she has a feeling it's better they not know the details. So she says quickly, "I'll have to Call back another Time. Talk to you Soon." Maybe capital letters don't travel well over telephone lines, because Maddie does not seem to get it.

"Bye," Maddie says. Gloom, on the other hand, travels just fine over thousands of miles of satellite connections.

The Clinic

WHAT WOULD DOLLY DO? Gloom or not, she would go forward, so that is what Dini is going to do. The only other person she knows in Swapnagiri who can talk to her about Dolly is Veeran the driver.

He's a fan, right? Dini thinks. Well, fans help each other out. That's how it is.

So when Veeran shows up to take Mom to the clinic the following morning, Dini volunteers to go along.

"Are you sure?" Mom says.

"Yes!" Dini says. "I mean, it's the whole reason we're here, right?"

"Right," says Mom.

"So I should check it out," Dini says. "And I can learn stuff."

"Stuff?" says Mom, raising an eyebrow but letting

Dini clamber into the Qualis ahead of her.

"Yes. About—um, vaccinations." Dini mumbles the last word in the hope that maybe Mom won't hear.

But Mom says, "Really?" as if she's surprised. Mom has started taking some medicine for her ear, so now she can hear again—too well, Dini thinks. They should make those medicines work at a more normal speed.

"Why don't we have a car?" Dini asks as Veeran revs the Qualis into gear and they shoot off down the red dirt road. "We had one in Maryland."

"We still have a car in Maryland," Mom reminds her, "and we don't really need one here. In fact, once I've figured out my way around here, I'm going to take the bus."

"Very fine buses here in Swapnagiri, madam," Veeran offers. "On time and all. Not like the big city, where everything is one big mess."

A bus lumbers past the Qualis. Buses do seem like a fine way to travel if you don't mind being pretty close to a whole lot of people. This one is full of riders carrying baskets and bundles and bulging bags.

Dolly could probably dance on top of that bus. That would make a terrific scene.

Then Dini sees something interesting sticking out of the bus window. Something metallic, big and round, and painted bright red.

"What's that?" she asks Mom.

"A cooking gas cylinder," Mom says. "We need to get one of those. That electric hot plate gets too hot. It's burning up everything we try to cook."

That's why all the food has been tasting a bit funny. Dini can't invite Dolly to dinner until they've fixed that.

Veeran slows down and honks a warning to a couple who have decided to cross the road right in front of the van. The woman is holding a chicken. For a moment Dini wonders if it is their pet, she is holding it so tenderly. But then she thinks, Maybe it's their dinner. She can tell that Swapnagiri is going to sharpen her guessing abilities.

The doctors and nurses in the clinic all fuss over Dini. "So tall." "And what are you writing in that notebook? You're taking notes on us?" They make her stand next to Mom so everyone can see how tall she is. "Very clever, too, probably," they say. "Just like your mother. You're going to be a doctor just like her?" Luckily, they don't seem to need Dini to answer any of their questions, so all she has to do is smile.

"Want the tour?" says Mom.

"Sure," Dini says.

The clinic is as full as the buses on the road. There are nurses taking people's blood pressure, and mothers getting their babies weighed.

A whole group of children have come to get their polio vaccine drops.

"This is my consulting room," Mom says, and parts a green curtain to let Dini through.

Women are waiting in the hallway to get shots for their babies, which makes Mom very happy, as she can then put them down in her book and they become part of this study she is doing on women and children and immunization and weight gain and whatnot.

"Hey," Dini says, "you have our pictures here." Dad and Dini are both on Mom's desk, in a folding frame. "And Maddie, too."

"I looked for a picture with just you in it," Mom says. "But you know what? Every picture I have of you, Maddie's in it too."

That is a five-year-old picture. Or maybe a six-year-old one, Dini can't remember. It is a nice feeling to think that Maddie is here. In this picture along with Dini, in Mom's clinic. Well, it would be even nicer if Maddie were still friends with her.

The women at the head of the line are already starting to edge into the room.

"Can I help?" Dini says. She can see that Mom needs to get to work. She does too, on her Dolly mission, but in the meantime those babies look so funny and squirmy that she wants to hang around and see what Mom does.

So she takes the pictures Mom hands her, of elephants and trees and a train, and distracts the babies so they don't see that the needle is coming along to jab them. She tries not to look at the needle herself, as she is not a big fan of needles. She tries to make noises like Priya, but she is better at waving pictures than creating sound effects.

Dini has to admit that Mom is a fast jabber. Some of those babies don't even know what hit them.

When the line starts to thin at last, Mom says, "You can go out if you like, sweetoo. You don't have to stick around in here all day." Dini glances

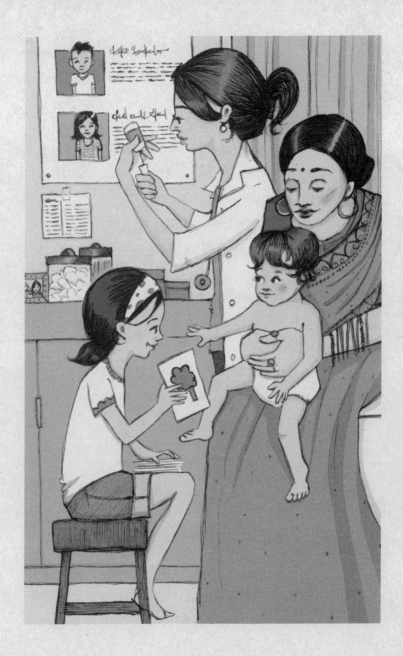

at the clock and sees that two hours have gone by and she hasn't yet had the chat with Veeran that she really came here for.

"Okay," she says, keeping it casual, not letting on that she is going on a most important mission. Make that in caps. A Most Important Mission. She goes off to find him.

In the back, where the Qualis is parked, Veeran the driver is checking its tire pressure. He is doing this with loving care, letting the tire go *pff-pfft* for a second, then stopping and checking again.

"Hello, Miss Nandini," he says, straightening up and patting his mustache into place. "So—how do you like our Swapnagiri?"

Dini tells him she likes it just fine, only she'd love it even better if she could find Dolly.

"She is not receiving any visitors," he says sadly. "That is what I've heard."

Me, Dini thinks. She'll see me. But she does not say that.

"Maybe she's retiring from the movies," he says.

"No!" Dini cries. "That's impossible. She can't do that." But then she thinks of that article in *Filmi Kumpnee* with that single word—"heartbreak"!—

on a line all by itself. And she worries.

Veeran says, "You should ask Mr. Chickoo Dev."

"The owner of Sunny Villa Estates?" Dini says, startled. There it is again. Coincidence. Or kismet. There seems to be quite a lot of it in Swapnagiri. More than in most places, Dini is sure.

"At one time," Veeran says, "Mr. Chickoo Dev was a very great friend of Miss Dolly Singh's. Some people even said . . . but who knows? Friendships come and go sometimes, with these famous filmi people."

Dolly's not like that, Dini thinks. She's loyal and true. In MJTJ when the villain is about to throw her best friend over the cliff, Dolly flings herself at him, screaming, "Throw me instead!" That's the kind of friend she is.

"I hope you find her," Veeran says. "I hope she's all right." He looks worried, which makes the ends of his mustache quiver.

"You're a true fan," says Dini, her heart over-flowing with the thought. One fan can see this quality in another. "And I'm sure you're a superfine mechanic, too," she adds generously.

Veeran reaches under the driver's seat of the

Qualis, pulls out a magazine, and gives it to Dini.

"*Filmi Kumpnee!*" says Dini, delighted. Maybe coincidence is just a little step in a plot leading to the next step.

Veeran nods his sideways yes nod. "You can keep it," he says to her.

Dini is surprised to find that when she nods back, her head is also moving sideways.

She spends the rest of the afternoon sitting on a bench in the little vegetable garden behind the clinic, where they grow all kinds of greens with bendy stalks and ruffly leaves, warty bitter melons, tomatoes, and spicy red hot peppers that curve like little daggers from their stems. And she reads the magazine.

From the "News 'n' Views" column of *Filmi Kumpnee: Your Magazine of the Stars*:

> Dolly Singh fans! Our hardworking *Filmi Kumpnee* reporters have been scouring the country for you.
>
> And the word is—ghayab.
>
> As in missing, disappeared, done a dimki.

Not in Bombay, our Dolly. Not in her Juhu top-floor flat. Not in her ground-floor-plus-ten-floors apartment building overlooking the Point. Not in any place that we have become accustomed to seeing her gracious and beautiful self.

But we are hot on her trail. And when we find her, you will be the first to know! We are alert. You be alert too. Keep your eye on this column.

For the first time ever, Dini realizes, she knows something about Dolly that the *Filmi Kumpnee* people do not know. And she is not about to tell them what she knows. Not in a hundred years.

Chapter Nineteen

Meena to Dolly

YOU ARE WELCOME STAY AS LNG AS YOU LIKE
DOLLY GOT YR LETTER LV MEENA

YOU GOT MY MSG DOLLY NO? TXTING FROM
MELBRNE AIRPRT CAN KEEP PHONE ON 5 MORE
MINUTES

YOURE NOT REPLYING TO MY MSGS DOLLY
SWEETIE WORRIED BACK SOON MEENA B.

Chapter Twenty

Blue Mountain School

WHILE MOM, with her perfect hearing now restored, is working hard to bring good health to the women and children of Swapnagiri, Dad and Dini pay a visit to the Blue Mountain School for an entrance test.

Well, Dad pays the visit. Dini has to take the test. "Why do I need to take a test?" Dini says.

"It's just the way they do things here," Dad says.

"What if I flunk it?" Dini says.

Dad gives her his oh-rani-are-you-nervous look. "You'll be fine," he says.

They follow a long, winding driveway past a playing field and an open space marked YOGA PAVILION to a round building where a woman in a green cotton sari is hurrying up to welcome everyone in. She is Mrs. Meena Balu, the principal. "You," she says, letting them in with a flourish of a wave, "must make yourselves at home. You must forgive me, I've just returned from overseas travel, so we're running a little late. Test takers, please, this way."

Dini follows her. So do a couple of other kids.

On their way to the testing room they pass a big flat-screen TV that is playing a video about the school. Wait! A face flashes by on the screen.

"Is that Dolly Singh?" Dini cries.

"You," murmurs the principal, "will see many distinguished guests here in this school." Dini can see that she is changing the subject on her. She wonders if Mrs. Balu ever begins a sentence with any other word but "you."

In the testing room half a dozen kids are sitting around waiting. Among them is Priya.

"Hi," Dini says.

"Hi," Priya replies, but she does not smile.

The test is not that difficult, but Dini is not paying attention very well because of that video. She's sure that was Dolly. She just can't figure out why. How is she connected to the school?

After Dini has answered math questions and science questions and reading comprehension questions, she has to write a two- to three-page essay on "How I Want to Change the World." She really throws herself into that because this is something she has thought about a lot. It has never occurred to Dini that anyone would really want to know her views on this subject of world-changing, but here in this school they are asking her.

So she writes about all the things she means to do someday when her life becomes perfect. They are good things, important things. Many kids have such ideas, it is true.

But here is the thing. Dini sets it all up like a movie script with herself as a character in the screenplay. It is a story about her growing up and getting really smart, which is bound to happen someday if she's patient enough. Then, in the screenplay, she goes on to make her life perfect so she can change the world, make it a place where problems are solved, true love wins, and dreams come true. It is complete with directions and all, the things that movie people call slug lines and parentheticals, all of which Dini knows from *Filmi Kumpnee*. When Mrs. Balu rings a little bell and announces that time is up, Dini is almost disappointed.

After the testing is done, everyone gathers back

in the main lobby of the circular building around a scale model of the school, while a teacher points out the various features of the campus. There is the main building, the trees, the winding pathway, the classroom complexes, the gym, the playing fields, and the yoga pavilion.

Maddie would like this school, Dini thinks, and she finds herself swept suddenly into a moment of missing Maddie. These moments seem to come upon her unexpectedly, a bit like jet lag.

"You will see," Mrs. Balu is saying, "that we have a small guesthouse in the back for special visitors. Sometimes we do parts of this orientation there, but it's currently occupied."

Refreshments follow, and Dini runs into Priya at the snack table. With her is the man who was driving the yellow car. Dini introduces Priya to Dad, and Priya introduces them both to the man. "My Uncle," says Priya.

"Just call me Chickoo," says Priya's uncle, extending a hand to Dad.

Mr. Chickoo Dev! He's Priya's uncle, with the face that looks as if it's all nose. Much shaking of hands follows, while Dad explains that they have just rented and moved into cottage number 6.

"I hope you're finding everything to your satisfaction," Mr. Chickoo Dev replies, most seriously.

Dad takes a breath. Dini is afraid that he is going to start talking about monkeys messing up the water-tank, so she takes charge of this conversation. "Everything," she says decidedly, "is just perfect." Dad closes his mouth.

"Excellent, excellent," says Chickoo Dev. He tells them how he inherited this huge, big tea estate from his great-aunty years ago and came to Swapnagiri, where he didn't know a soul. Dini has to admit that while Chickoo Dev seems like a nice man, he is not completely fascinating.

But suddenly, while he's talking about this stuff, and Dad is nodding and agreeing with him about the rupee-euro exchange and the price of tea, Dini notices something. Chickoo Dev's nose, which looked a little . . . well, big the last time Dini saw it, now seems perfectly fine for his face. It is an honest sort of face otherwise—not every face has to fascinate, after all. It is crowned with a mop of dark hair that gives it a sensitive look. He laughs, and a person could forget that nose.

He gives Dad his phone number and says if they need any help, just ask. "How nice," he says, "that Nandini and Priya will be in school together."

Priya and Dini look warily at each other.

"How do you like Swapnagiri?" says Chickoo Dev to Dad.

Dad says that his wife, Dini's mom, has dreamed of coming here for years and years. "And I'm so glad she brought us," he says. "It's a beautiful part of the country."

"Perfect for movies," Dini says. She can't help herself. It's just that the Dini Meets Dolly movie is never too far from her thoughts.

Priya scowls. She makes a hissy noise that sounds like the complaint of a snake that has just eaten something disagreeable.

"My daughter's a big movie fan," Dad says, as if an apology is needed.

Priya glares. Yes, that is definitely a glare.

Dini flounders on because she has started this up, so she has to keep going. She tells Chickoo Dev about how she dreamed of Dolly Singh dancing through the tea-gardens the very first day they came to Swapnagiri.

Chickoo Dev sighs. He stays silent so long that Dini thinks perhaps he has fallen asleep standing right there, but at last he says, "That was my dream also."

Really? He is a fan too! But she can tell from his face that something is wrong. Something is the matter with his fan dream.

"I wanted her to shoot this movie right here." He waves at the hillside, covered with bright green tea bushes. "Only she . . . how can I say it? She backed out of the agreement."

"We are Not," says Priya, who has quit being a snake and is now speaking again, "on Talking Terms with that Dolly Person, are we, Chickoo Uncle?" She draws a breath in, *click-click*, like a door locking.

Priya's uncle Chickoo Dev looks very, very sad.

"Why?" Dini says.

"Nandu!" Dad frowns at her. He is embarrassed by her directness, no doubt, but she doesn't care. If she isn't direct, no one is going to be. It's very clear that direct talking is precisely what is needed at this moment.

"Forgive me, I'm not at liberty to disclose," murmurs Chickoo Uncle.

"Quite understandable," Dad murmurs back, shooting Dini a look. A warning look. A stop-being-nosy-right-now look.

Understandable? Not at liberty? Maybe Dad understands, but Dini certainly doesn't. All this time she has been plotting in her notebook the story lines that could possibly lead her to Dolly, but this is not one she has anticipated. Now what is she supposed to do?

Chapter Twenty-one

Lal

KREER! KOOCH! KRAAR! The sorting machine in the post office in Mumbai has stopped and will not start again.

"It's broken," someone says.

"Impossible," snaps the postmaster. "This is a brand-new imported machine recommended by our India Post collaborators in the United States of America. How can it be broken?"

"Sir, sorry sir, but it's b-broken," says Lal the postal carrier, his uniform crackling anxiously as he sticks his head into the sorting room. He has been waiting patiently for his bag but he simply cannot compromise any longer the motto of India Post ("Speed and efficiency").

"Did someone manhandle this machine?" roars the postmaster. "Did one of you rascals feed it a lunch chapati instead of a letter, or what?"

All the mail now has to be sorted by hand. This is a very big job. Everyone has to join in, even Lal, even though he has something else on his mind.

"Sir," says Lal, trying to make himself heard over the surge of voices and the chaos of hands shuffling envelopes.

But the postmaster is not about to allow any idle chatter. "Not now, young man," he says severely. "Can't you see we are in the middle of a crisis? Everybody must sit and sort, that's right! Buck up and buckle down for the sake of India Post and Mother India, jai hind!"

The postmaster salutes. He is always deeply moved whenever he thinks that his post office is working for India's greater good and glory. "SIT!" he bellows. "SORT!"

So Lal sits and sorts, sits and sorts. As he is sitting and sorting, an envelope in the Speed Post pile catches his eye. It is white, decorated with silver flowers. A fussy envelope, the kind used by a person who is used to throwing money away on envelopes.

There it is again, that thing that most people would call coincidence. Lal prefers to think of it as kismet. Some people would say kismet means fate, but really it is a far more beautiful idea—it is the idea that in spite of all the obstacles, some things are meant to be.

The Speed Post envelope is addressed to one Mr. Soli Dustup of Starlite Studios, with an address in Cuffe Parade, which as everyone knows is where many, many movie-studio-type people live. The stars, of course, all have top-floor places overlooking the Point and seaside houses on Juhu Beach. But the people who run the business, they live in Cuffe Parade.

Now Lal notes that Dolly Singh—that very same Dolly Singh—is the sender of this letter in the superfine envelope. And she is sending it from somewhere that is far from Mumbai. The cancellation is a little blurry, but Lal can make out the name of the town where this letter was mailed. Swapnagiri!

Lal thinks a bit. He remembers from his geography classes in Byculla Municipal School Number 187 that Swapnagiri town is in the Blue Mountains of the south. He has always wanted to go there. He has heard that the air is so fresh in those hills that you can ride a bicycle up and down all day and not feel in the least tired.

He is pleased at all the thinking this letter has generated. There is something satisfying about being the person to handle letters that have traveled so far, to take them to their proper destination. He has not forgotten the day that another letter arrived all the way from America with no PIN code, no proper address even. He has not forgotten that he, Lal, helped to get that letter to the correct address.

"Lal," growls the postmaster, "are you going to eat that letter or put it in a delivery bag?" For the first time since he started this job six months ago, Lal notices how very canine the postmaster is. He is an attack dog employed to guard the mail. He never speaks. He growls, howls, roars, barks, snaps. Does he also bite?

"S-sir, no sir, I mean, yes sir," says Lal, and he drops the letter into its right and proper bag.

Then he sets out on his round. About halfway through his route it is his pleasant task to deliver that Speed Post letter to Mr. Soli Dustup of Cuffe Parade.

Mr. Dustup is still in his green striped pajamas that day. This is not because he overslept. In fact, all night he was sleepless. As a result, he is exhausted and has spent the day brooding over endless cups of coffee as bitter as his mood.

When Lal rings the doorbell (this letter being one of those registered affairs that call for a recipient's signature), Mr. Dustup flings the door open, his other hand clutched to his head, and begs, "Please. Stop that racket."

"S-so-sorry, sir," Lal says, and hands him the Speed Post letter. It does not escape Lal's notice, for he is a keen observer of human nature, that Mr. Dustup grabs the letter as if he is a drowning man and it is a lifeboat.

It gladdens Lal immensely to be delivering such necessary and important mail, and he goes on his way, whistling. Little does he know the tragedy he is leaving in his wake.

Chapter Twenty-two

The Electric Car

THE NEXT DAY DINI AND DAD take the bus into town to a bakery Dad knows of on Blue Mountain Road. Mom is an advocate of fruit instead of sugary foods, so Dad and Dini are allies when it comes to seeking out things like chocolate and cookies.

"We'll just get a little something," Dad says as they get off the bus.

Dini is looking forward to that little something. Maybe a little something with chocolate in it. But they can't get anything at all because the bakery is closed. A big sign on the front door says, BACK TOMORROW. CHEERY-BYE.

"Oh dear," Dad says. "Too bad."

Dini stares sadly at the sign. The cakes and pastries in the window look wonderful. They look rich and chocolaty. It is just another thing that is not going according to plan. Here she is in the same town as Dolly, and the trail has gone, as they say in mystery fillums, cold.

And Maddie, who should be her ally and friend, is not happy. She's mad with Dini because she thinks Dini is making scads of friends and having a wonderful time in India without her. This Priya girl, who doesn't even know Dini, is mad with her. And now the bakery that is the only place in Swapnagiri to get chocolate is closed. Really, life is more complicated than any movie that Dini can imagine.

Almost without thinking, she makes a noise like a buzzy bird, but it's not anywhere near as good as Priya's bird sound.

A soft hiss floats down in reply. Dini looks up, startled.

Is that Priya on the roof of the bakery?

No, it is a monkey.

The monkey throws a half-eaten marigold down and misses Dini by inches.

"Cheery-bye to you," Dini says gloomily.

"Sorry, Nandu," says Dad. "I guess this turned out to be a wild-goose chase."

Dini takes a deep breath. There's that Nandu

name again. "Dad," she says. "Dini—okay? Please?"

"Oh, right," Dad says. "I keep forgetting. All right, Dini. . . ."

"Thanks, Dad."

Dad puts his hand on Dini's head and rumples her hair. Maybe one day she will pick the perfect moment to tell him that he needs to stop doing that. But two of these growing-up things in one day is probably too much for him to handle.

Dad says, "Want to walk down to the garage?"

"Sure," Dini says.

It turns out that Veeran, the driver of the clinic's white Qualis, works a second job every other day as a mechanic at the Tune-and-Fix Garage ("You Bring, We Fix"), on the east end of Blue Mountain Road. And Veeran has asked Dad to come help him with something.

Sure enough, they find Veeran at the Tune-and-Fix, with his feet sticking out from under a car.

He slides out and wipes a bit of grease off his face with a rag. "Vanakkam," he greets them, which Dini has learned by now is Tamil for "hello" or "welcome" or some combination. He says to Dad, "This is the car, sir. Electric car, and this is the special diagnostic computer." His mustache droops.

But Dini has no time for computers because this car in front of her is not just any car. "I've seen that car before!" she cries.

Sure enough, Veeran says, "This is Mr. Chickoo Dev's car."

"Is something wrong with it?" Dini asks.

"Everything is new and beautiful about this car," says Veeran sadly. "Nice engine, new batteries and all, excellent mileage. Warranty has only just expired. But when you drive it, aaah, there's this noise, this noise!" He slaps his hand against his forehead. "It will not go away. I have looked everywhere to see what could be making it, but no luck. So that's why I thought, maybe something is wrong with the new diagnostic computer."

"What kind of noise?" Dini asks.

"Rattling noise," says Veeran, "and sometimes the radio seems to come on, but when I check it, it's always off. So how can the computer say everything is fine?"

Dad says, "Let me take a look." And he starts to mouse around the screen of the computer that sits on a desk in the garage. Dad is never so happy as

when he is mousing around the screen of some computer, trying to fix a problem. Dini can see that Dad feels about computers the way Veeran does about cars. And the way I do about Dolly, Dini thinks in surprise. Never before has she thought that worrying about Dolly is a job for her, but it is beginning to feel that way.

Veeran throws his hands up in the air, finding no words able to express how he feels about that noise. "Sir, it's my reputation, you see. I've just now completed the special training to get my mechanic's license for this brand-new line of electric cars. If I can't find out what the problem is . . ." He hangs his head.

Dini can see that Veeran is really worried about Mr. Chickoo Dev's car, and now he thinks maybe he is not a superfine mechanic because he can't fix this problem. What a lot of trouble that noise is causing.

And now Dini sees something that only those who listen-listen, look-look, can understand. Open one problem up, like the hood of a car, and you may find another problem waiting to be solved. Try opening that one up and you are likely to find several dozen others just waiting to get in your way. It is all very depressing.

Dad runs a couple of programs on the garage's diagnostic computer and pronounces it to be perfectly fine, no bugs at all. "It's the car," he says, "it must be."

They leave Veeran standing sadly in the doorway of the Tune-and-Fix Garage ("You Bring, We Fix").

In the bus on the way back Dini plots out some ways this could play out. Veeran could find something dangerously wrong with the yellow car, but it comes to him only after Chickoo Uncle's taken the car back and is driving it away into the sunset. Veeran could chase after him in the white Qualis, flag him down, and get him out of the car before it explodes, thus saving Chickoo Uncle's life. Dolly could hear of it and come running to Chickoo Uncle's side. That is one option.

But will all these people *do* these things the way the story needs them to? *WWDD?* Dini asks herself. What Would Dolly Do? Dolly would get everyone to make it all work somehow, wouldn't she? None of those *Filmi Kumpnee* articles ever told Dini just how much hard work it is to plot out a story when the people who are in it do not want to cooperate.

All the way back down the road to Sunny Villa, the bus picks up passengers—a group of twelve people from baby to grandpa who all look enough like one another that you know they are family, a woman with shopping bags full of tea, a man with a little black-and-white baby goat in his arms.

The goat looks right into Dini's face and gives a little bleat. It seems as if it is telling her to cheer up and hang in there. She feels unreasonably like crying, and so she blinks to stop herself. The goat blinks back. It has the kind of face that makes a person smile, so small, with its baby fuzz still silky on it. An encouraging sort of face.

Chapter Twenty-three

Missing Maddie

"HOW'S MY GIRL?" says Mom, all bright and chirpy after what has undoubtedly been a happy, healthful day at the clinic. They are sitting together in the tiny garden outside Sunny Villa cottage number 6, listening to some rather loud overlapping sounds drifting on the evening breeze. Dini folds her legs under her and rests her chin on the wide arm of the chair.

"Okay," she says.

"Only okay?" Mom switches to concern.

Dini spent all afternoon waiting for a time that she could call Maddie without waking her up. When the time came and she called, the line was busy. How could Maddie's phone line be busy? Who could she possibly be talking to? "Okay" will have to do.

"Networking problems," Dad explains. Dini

looks at him to see if he's joking, but he seems to be perfectly serious.

"I'm sorry," Mom says. "Relax. It'll all work out. Just enjoy this beautiful view."

"What, the road?" Dini says. A road, moreover, on which there has not been any traffic to speak of, not since a bunch of goats ran by all of fifteen minutes ago with a goatherd chasing after them. A maddeningly empty road.

Mom and Dad look at each other over Dini's head. Dini rolls her eyes.

"Oh, sweetoo," says Mom. "It's hard on you, I know."

"If I could just find Dolly," says Dini, "then at least I'd be . . . you know . . ." She's not quite sure what she means to say. She just knows that finding Dolly was never so important.

"Hmm," Dad says. "That's a tough job you've set yourself there. Needle in a haystack."

Mom reaches out and pats Dad's arm, which for some reason makes Dad stop talking. They look at each other again, which makes Dini want to get up and stomp into the house, only she's got pins and needles in her right leg from having it folded under her for too long, so stomping is out of the question.

Mom says, "I know what. You should send Maddie something from here. Something special."

"What a good idea," Dad says.

Dini knows what she would like to send Maddie. A picture of Dolly, with Dolly's glorious, swirling signature across the front, angled just right, in glittery green ink. That's what she'd like to send. It would make everything perfect once more. She can almost hear Maddie's excited scream when she gets it. Almost, but not really.

Because finding Dolly is turning out to be as daunting a task as finding that thing that's making the noise in Mr. Chickoo Dev's car.

Still, when all the lights are out and Dini is lying in bed trying to fall asleep, Mom's idea sinks in. It's not a bad idea. Send her something special.

Something special. What can Dini send her? Watching the moonlight streak across the wall, and listening to some night bird shrieking its head off in the distance, Dini considers this new question.

She cannot send Maddie a tea bush, or a monkey,

or a house with funny-looking shutters that look like eyelashes.

Maddie likes chocolate. But Dini is not sure they let you send chocolate in the mail, and anyway, the mail will take too long. She wants to send something now.

She even gets up and turns on the light and looks in her notebook, but there is no inspiration there. She would like to send Maddie the news that she has found Dolly and plot-fixed her broken heart, but that has not yet happened.

She hums a Dolly tune, and in the middle of the bit that goes, "Oh-my-heart-oh-my-heart, oh my hea-art," she falls asleep.

Chapter Twenty-four

Jug-Handle-Ears?

IN MUMBAI THAT ALL the filmi people still call Bombay, in that twelfth-floor apartment where his nimble brain dreams up new fillum projects, Mr. Soli Dustup of Starlite Studios is turning purple in the face.

He is turning purple because he has just received a letter. That is not all. First his ears were assaulted by the harsh jangle of the doorbell, rung by a postal worker who had no business looking as cheerful as he did. Then he had to sign for this letter, which was sent by Speed Post. In Mr. Dustup's opinion, signing for this letter was like paying a camera crew who then turned around and shot the movie for your competition. Because when he opened and read the letter, it turned out to be a most insulting letter, a letter that no sensitive human being ought to be subjected to.

June 17

Dear Mr. Jug-Handle-Ears Dustup.

He is a potato nose. And I am so upset I could spit in your eye! How could you cancel my contract Just because His Royal Highness Mr. Chickoo Dev loves his CAR more than ME?

You can kiss your advance good-bye. I am not returning a paisa.

D. Singh

"Jug...jug-handle?" splutters Mr. Dustup. He touches his right ear gingerly. It is still there on the side of his head as it has always been. It is not that big. Is it?

"Star or no star," he mutters, "this time I swear she has gone too far."

In more than one way, he thinks darkly. Swapnagiri is a three-hour flight away, and an hour and a half after that on a winding mountain road, and Mr. Soli Dustup has a delicate constitution. The thought of his stomach being buffeted about in a car that is careening around steep mountain bends—that thought makes him turn from purple to puce.

Chapter Twenty-five

Power Failure

DINI FLIPS THROUGH the children's section of the newspaper. "Kids' Korner," it says. It has comics and riddles and a maze. She reads a riddle: "What goes up when the rain comes down? Answer: Umbrellas." Not very funny, Dini thinks.

She traces a path through the maze and contemplates the mess she has made of what was once a plan. Bump, her finger runs into a maze wall. She tries another way. Bump—another wall.

It's been a waste of a day. It's been raining, for one thing, so she can't even go out. How many times can she rearrange her green and silver stripy collection of bags and scarves and bangles and things? She wonders moodily why you are supposed to carry out a plan, anyway. Where do you carry it out to, and what do you do with it once you are there? No one ever tells you things like that. "Oh, just make a plan," they say, "and carry it out." Now Dini has carried her plan out, all the way out to India, and what is the use of that? Where does that leave this so-called plan? Dini thinks. In the water-tank after the monkeys have been through, that's where.

She turns the paper over to the headlines.

"Horses respond to trainer's thoughts," says the Indian Express. It seems there is a new way to train horses. You stand in front of the horse and you think, Come here. And it does. You think, Go away, and it does. The trainers are very excited about this and are teaching everyone they can find how to train horses this way.

Dini thinks, Maybe that would work if Dolly was a horse, but she is not. She sits and thinks about how nothing is working the way it's supposed to, when the sky outside does a quick scene change. The clouds part. The sun plunks down behind the hills in a sudden blaze of orange.

That reminds Dini of the sunset in MJTJ, which in turn pops an idea into her mind. Those MJTJ scenes are pure magic, Dini thinks, and now she knows what she can send Maddie. It is the perfect gift.

She tosses the newspaper aside and runs to turn the computer on. Now to the *Filmi Kumpnee* site, with its download page. "All Songs, All Free, All the Time," says the banner. She'll send Maddie a Dolly song.

Not only is it the perfect gift, but it will convey the perfect message. It will say, *You are still my friend.* Songs can say things like this, even when these things are not in the lyrics.

But oh, the twists and turns of fate. There is a problem with the *Filmi Kumpnee* songs page. With so many options next to each song title, all having to do with kilobytes and seconds and modem speeds and types, Dini soon realizes she's clueless. How does a person download a song when these buttons are staring back at her from the screen and she has no idea which one to click?

"What are you doing sitting in the dark?" Dad comes in, reaching for the light switch. The light comes on extra bright, then flickers and goes out. Now it is even darker than it was before.

"Oh no!" Dini says. "What happened? I wanted to send Maddie a song."

"Can't send anything now," Mom says. "Power failure."

Dad clicks the table lamp switch back and forth. Nothing.

"Nobody move," Mom says. "Some very smart person gave me a gift that'll come in really handy in this emergency." She gropes her way to the kitchen and comes back cranking a handle on something. The something is the flashlight Dad bought in Maryland, the one that twenty cranks will power for five minutes.

"That was a smart person," Dad says in a pleased voice.

"Told you," Mom says. She cranks and cranks, and soon there is enough light to locate matches, and one of the candles that Sampy brought them. The crack of a match later, the candle splays the shadows of three people all over the walls.

Maybe it is those shadows. Maybe it is the very high corners of this room, where the walls meet and the light can't reach. Maybe it is Mom and Dad looking so pleased with themselves about the flashlight that is all green and no batteries. Maybe it is all those things, and the computer that can no longer send anything zinging around the world. But suddenly, all of Dini's optimism, which she has tried so hard to preserve, just falls away from her like so many loose rocks tumbling down a hillside.

"Everything is all wrong," she bursts out.

"Oh dear," says Mom.

"Why?" says Dad. "What's wrong with my favorite daughter?"

"Everything!" Dini says, and she doesn't even feel cheery enough to point out, as she would normally do, that she is his only daughter. "At this rate I'm not going to have any friends left."

"Oh, don't say that, my rani," says Dad. "I'll be your friend."

"Da-ad," says Dini. "No offense, but you're not the right person for that job."

Mom says, "Maddie's still your friend."

"I don't know!" Dini wails. And she tells them the thing she has been carrying around inside her ever since it happened. How Maddie thinks Priya is Dini's friend but she's not, and how no one—no one—is going to help Dini find Dolly. "And now I can't even send Maddie a Dolly song because of the stupid electricity!"

The light blazes back on. "Oh!" Dini runs across the room to the computer.

"Uh, rani," Dad says. "You can't send her an audio file anyway." He goes on about some bug in the audio-file-transfer-thingy that he needs to fix. He does not say "thingy," but Dini can't be bothered trying to unravel Dad's computer talk.

She is giving up and slumping into the sofa when she spots something else. "And there's a crack in the ceiling," she says.

Her parents peer up, blinking in the sudden brightness.

"That's not a problem," says Dad. "We'll just tell Mr. Dev, and he'll send someone to fix it."

"Sweetie," says Mom, "change is always difficult. Just give it some time."

Dini says nothing.

"I think," says Mom, "that we're all doing really well. We're settling into this house. Daddy has his fast network all set up. Soon you'll start school, and you'll feel so much better."

"That's right," Dad says. "It's all about connectivity."

Dini has no idea what he is talking about.

Dad looks up at the ceiling, the thing he does whenever he has something important to say and is about to use up quite a few words to say it. In their house in Maryland there was that place above the kitchen door that he always looked at for this purpose, where the line of the doorframe and the level of the ceiling above it were a tiny bit off and not quite parallel to each other. This was enough to spark a speech. Here, Dini sees, it is that crack in the ceiling she just spotted.

"Connectivity," Dad says, as if he has just invented the word. He proceeds to talk at length about bits, bytes, and data streams.

Mom reminds Dad that it is his turn to cook dinner. "No gas cylinder yet," Dad complains. "I keep burning everything on that little electric hot plate."

"We'll help you," Mom says. "We can put some rice on. I think there's some leftover egg curry in the fridge."

"It's burned," Dad says sadly. "It got stuck to the bottom of the pan."

If there were a camera handy sometime later, it would be zooming in on three tired people eating slightly scorched egg curry along with a little singed rice.

Chapter Twenty-six

Lal and the Postmaster

IT IS A TOUGH DAY for Lal at the Mumbai (used to be called Bombay) post office. Lal is by nature a mild-mannered young man. But now he has to raise an important matter with his boss, the postmaster. This is because Lal's mother, who puts the starch into his crackly uniform, has just done another wonderful, motherly thing. She has found him a wife. This is why he has to speak up, even if the postmaster is in the middle of yet another crisis.

The postmaster's crisis on this day has to do with this wretched machine that is turning out to be a headache of such proportions that all the postmaster's previous headaches (and he has had many of them) fade to nothing in comparison.

The machine has begun to work now, where before it was not working at all. But it is now sorting all the mail in reverse PIN code order, so that items intended for, say, the outskirts of Delhi (110097) end up on some mountainside in Arunachal Pradesh (790011). This is a colossal problem. In spite of having this high-tech wonder right here, the postmaster now has to make all his workers sort all the mail by hand. Even the lowly letter carriers have to pitch in because this high-tech wonder has turned out to have its brain in backward.

But although the postmaster may not agree, some things are more important than even a broken India Post machine.

Lal clears his throat. "Sir," he says, "I am . . . I am happy to announce, sir, that I will be getting married, sir, very . . . sh-shortly."

Everyone claps and cheers—everyone but the postmaster.

"Married?" howls the postmaster.

Lal jumps straight up in the air from shock. The clapping ceases abruptly.

"Married!" the postmaster growls. "Have you even worked here four months yet?"

"S-s-sir, more than four. Six months, s-s-sir, yes, sir," stammers poor Lal.

"Don't you know that our busy summer postal season is not over yet? You'll be wanting leave, I suppose!"

Lal blinks. He bows his head. But he says nothing. The postmaster may not be happy about it, but Lal is getting married just the same.

The postmaster takes a deep breath. He closes his eyes. He seems to be mumbling a small prayer to himself. "All right, all right," he says at last, calming down. "I'll deal with you later. Now, everyone get back to work!"

Lal relaxes. It seems the postmaster may howl and growl, but he does not bite after all.

Soon the letters are sorted—manually, once again. "This is the downside of technology," snarls the postmaster. "When it works, it's magic, but once it fails—how tragic!"

No one dares to point out to him that he is now barking in rhymes.

Soon the postmaster goes off to write a letter of his own, to the chief of India Post. He will complain about the new machine. It may have been recommended by the United States Postal Service experts, he will say, but it is breaking down over and over again, even when he has personally made certain that no one has fed it lunch chapatis instead of letters.

Someone ventures to say, "Congratulations, Lal."

Lal allows himself to beam a little. He is feeling quite beamy inside, even if he dare not show that beaminess to the postmaster.

Someone else asks, "So . . . where are you going on your honeymoon, Lal? Darjeeling? Kashmir?"

Lal hesitates. Then, on the spot, that very minute, he makes up his mind. He will of course ask his intended bride what she thinks, but he is certain she will agree with this choice. How can she not? She is also a Dolly fan, and maybe . . . who knows? If Dolly is still in that beautiful place, they may catch a glimpse of her. That will be a memory they will hold in their hearts for the rest of their lives.

"Swapnagiri," he says.

He murmurs it a few more times to himself as he sets off on his route. Swapnagiri. Even the name, meaning "dream mountain," feels magical.

Lal hums a little song under his breath as he cycles along the busy streets with his bags of mail, his uniform crackling with happiness.

Chapter Twenty-seven

Connectivity

SLEEP IS A MAGICAL THING. Dini goes to sleep on Wednesday night with the rain cloud of her problems hanging over her head. On Thursday morning, when she wakes up bright and early, they have not gone away. Not exactly. But something has changed. It is as if something has come up when the rain came down. Perhaps, as the riddle in the paper said, that something is an umbrella.

Sleep has given Techie Dad extra energy too, it appears. He pushes his chair back from the computer desk and stands up, takes a contented sip from his coffee cup. "Hey, hey, hey," he says. "Guess what?"

"What?" she says.

"Got it!" says Dad. "There!"

"Where?" says Dini.

"Listen," Dad says. He hits a key, and flute music

wafts out into the room. "I fixed that pesky audio problem."

Dini's heart, the one that has been sinking a bit lately, now grows wings and does a little dance.

"Wait," she says. "Does that mean I can send Maddie a Dolly song file?"

"Sure," says Dad. "Why not?"

So Dini shows him the web page with the buttons that stumped her last night.

And this is the beauty of fast networks. In a matter of fifteen minutes three perfect files (all songs from MJTJ, and Dini knows Maddie doesn't have them yet) are whizzing around the world to hurraymaddie@globenet.link.

They are not happy songs, Dini is well aware. "If I Call You, Will You Come?" "No One Knows Where My House Is." "Only Clear Skies Will Cure a Broken Heart." Still, they are giving Maddie that message—that you-are-my-friend message.

Dini just hopes Maddie will get this. The Maddie she knew would have gotten it. But she, Dini, would have been there to make sure of that. To explain such subtle but important messages. To point out how the things you don't say still matter. In fact, to do all those things that Dolly does in her movies when people don't get a point that needs to be understood.

It is a real pain to know what needs to happen but not be there to make sure it does.

Chapter Twenty-eight

Letters Flying Back and Forth

June 19

Dolly, are you still here? Are you all right?

Chickoo

June 20

Still here.

All right? What is all right? Nothing is all right!

How could you even think to ask such a question?

I am bereft and bemused. I am perplexed and put out.

Once I had dreams. Now they are all dumped down the hillside.

Chickoo, how could you?

June 21

How could I what? Dolly, what did I do? I don't understand. You're the one who threw a perfectly good diamond ring away.

June 22

You care more about that car than me. And more about that diamond.

June 23

It was a very expensive diamond. You don't understand. I am trying to carry on as usual, getting Priya admitted to school, managing the estate. But my heart is heavy.

June 24

I do, believe me. I understand all too well. Your
heart hurts more for that car than it ever did for
me. These are tears, Chickoo, all over this letter.
I am hapless and hopeless.

Chapter Twenty-nine

Dreamy Cakes

THAT AFTERNOON Dad's cell phone rings. "Heee-llo?" he says. Then he says, "Yes," and, "Oh, that's very good news," and, "Thank you, we will. How kind of you."

"Who's that?" Dini asks.

"Your friend Priya's uncle, Mr. Chickoo Dev," Dad says. "He was at the Blue Mountain School checking on Priya's admission."

"And?" says Dini. Blech. What if Priya got into the Blue Mountain School and she, Dini, did not? She has to go to school, doesn't she? She can see herself having to be here for two years without a school, growing stupider and stupider until her brain just comes to a screeching halt. She has never even thought before about how important school is in a kid's life.

But Dad is smiling. "They told him in the school

office that the letters are on their way," he says, "but he also saw the names of new students posted on the school bulletin board."

"And?" says Dini. Can't he get to the point?

"You and Priya both got in," he says, "and Chickoo Dev has invited us to meet them at Dreamycakes Bakery for a plate of curry puffs and something chocolaty."

"And you said yes?"

"Of course I said yes," Dad says. "Why?"

Dini shakes her head.

"I thought you wanted to go to Dreamycakes," says Dad, looking hurt.

Well, Dini did. Does. And she does not want to hurt Dad's feelings. But . . . but . . . but . . . "Dad," she says, "how can I say this? Priya doesn't like me."

"Of course she does," says Dad, getting into cheery-happy mode. "How can she not like you?"

Dini can think of a dozen ways, but listing them won't do any good. "She just doesn't."

But Dad only grins and plants a kiss on Dini's head. "Come on. Let bygones be bygones. Every day is a new day. Give her a chance to turn over a new leaf." He stops, looking very pleased at having come up with so many nifty phrases in a single breath. He says, "Well? Are you coming?"

Dini groans. She wants to go. She doesn't. Yes. No. Oh, she can't stand it when things push-pull her like this.

Dad is waiting patiently for her reply. And Dini certainly knows what it's like to wait patiently for things to happen when you have a plan and are hoping to carry it out. So, "Okay," she says at last. "Let's go."

Dreamycakes, the only bakery in Swapnagiri, is open on this fine Thursday afternoon.

While they are waiting for Chickoo Uncle and Priya to show up, Dad tells the owner how he and Dini came by earlier in the week, but it was closed.

"So very sorry," says the owner, Mr. Mani, as he sees them to a table by the window. "I had to go to the post office to send off a most important letter."

The letter, it seems, was to the people at Guinness World Records.

"Guinness World Records?" Dini says. That does sound important.

"It is a long story," says Mr. Mani, settling down to tell it.

Mr. Mani's great-grandfather was a cook in the Indian Army. He traveled all over India with his regiment. He even cooked on the front lines for the troops.

But his true passion was the creation of superlight cakes and superfine chocolate confections, and so he had a secret dream—he dreamed of getting into the Guinness World Records book by baking the biggest chocolate cake in the world.

"Wow!" Dini can see that cake. It would have to be pictured in a straight shot, no fancy angles needed, maybe against some really nice background. Outdoors, definitely.

"Alas," says Mr. Mani, breaking into this pleasant image. "His effort failed. Only minutes before the Guinness representative arrived to check the size and weight of his cake, it was unfortunately eaten by a troop of ravenous monkeys who broke into the bakery and cleaned out every last crumb."

"Oh no!" Dini cries. This is a tragic twist. Monkeys!

Such is the power of family legend, it seems, that even today the mere sight of a monkey is enough to make Mr. Mani fall into a massive weeping panic.

Dini thinks it best not to tell Mr. Mani about that monkey that hissed at her from the roof.

In any case, Mr. Mani has concluded his sad story and is ready to move to the next scene. He says, "Well, that was all a long time ago, a very long time. My cake—well, we shall see. But here are your friends, I think." And waving at the door, which is opening at that very moment, Mr. Mani goes off to bring out his samples of the day's specials.

Here indeed are Priya and her uncle, one of them smiling, one of them not so smiling.

"So," says Chickoo Uncle. "Congratulations, you two. You are now going to be classmates."

"Yes," says Dini.

"Yes," says Priya.

"Let bygones be bygones, that's what I say," says Chickoo Uncle.

Does he really mean that? Maybe there is hope for the Dolly-Chickoo story line after all.

"That's exactly what *I* say too," says Dad, clearly delighted to find a fellow lover of nifty expressions. "Sit down, sit down."

Priya and Chickoo Uncle sit down with Dini and Dad at the table by the window. They all sample the curry puffs. Delicious. They sample the chocolate cake. Delectable. They order plates of each, along with some milk shakes (choice of chocolate and rose petal).

Their orders arrive. For a while Dreamycakes Bakery is filled with the musical sounds of chewing and swallowing, and with murmurs of appreciation.

Priya says, "Know what the Secret curry puff Ingredient is?"

Dini nibbles. "Onion?" she ventures. "Potatoes?"

"Nope," Priya says. "Try again."

"Flour?"

"Nope."

"Butter?"

"Chocolate," Priya says. "Everything they make here has Chocolate in it."

Dini says, "Really? Chocolate?" She tries another bite. "Hmm, now I can taste it. It's good." It is surprisingly good, in fact. You wouldn't think chocolate and potatoes would work well together at all, but they do.

"My friend Maddie would like this," Dini says. "She really likes chocolate."

"I Like it Sometimes," Priya says, sipping at her rose petal milk shake, which she has ordered without chocolate.

"And how is your car doing?" Dad says to Chickoo Uncle. Just making conversation, Dini can see.

Priya groans. That is apparently not a good question to ask.

"The noise is worse," Chickoo Uncle says sadly. "Now the songs are becoming slow and mournful."

"Songs?" Dini is puzzled. "The car's singing to you?"

"Yes," Chickoo Uncle says, and he is sounding slow and mournful too. "And rattling. We looked under the hood. We checked the radio connections. But still it's singing. And the rattling and clanking and clunking are still there."

"Very puzzling," says Dad.

"It's my worst nightmare," says Mr. Chickoo Dev.

Dini says, "What songs is the car playing?"

Priya makes a long hissing sound like an unhappy snake. "Dolly songs," she says, "every single one."

From the look on Chickoo Uncle's face, Dini realizes she didn't get what he meant about bygones being bygones. It looks as though he would like

Dolly songs to be bygones in his life.

"How did you like those curry puffs?" Mr. Mani asks as they pay their bill at the counter.

They assure him the curry puffs were great. And they are. They are delicious. Delectable. The curry puffs are not the problem at all.

Chapter Thirty

There's Maddie!

OH, WHAT A DAY IT'S BEEN, with song files and chocolate and mystery noises all clamoring for attention! Dini checks her e-mail that evening to make sure Maddie's received her songs. She has. It seems from her e-mail message that Maddie is willing to let bygones turn into dance steps.

From: hurraymaddie@globenet.link

To: dini@swpn.com.in

Subject: Songs

Date: Wednesday, June 23, 2010, 21:36:03 EDT

Thank you thank you thank you. How nice of you to send me those dancey Dolly songs. My feet have been tap-tap-tapping all day. P.S. Have you found her yet?

From: dini@swpn.com.in

To: hurraymaddie@globenet.link

Subject: Re: Songs

Date: Thursday, June 24, 2010, 18:09:53 IST

Maddie I'm so glad you liked them. No Dolly yet.

Any ideas?

She gets a reply so swiftly it makes her dizzy. She looks at the time on the e-mail header, and it is as if Maddie has sent her reply before Dini even sent out her question. This is what happens when you are on opposite sides of the world and nearly a dozen time zones apart. It is a magical thing.

From: hurraymaddie@globenet.link

To: dini@swpn.com.in

Subject: Re: Songs

Date: Thursday, June 24, 2010, 08:42:37 EDT

Throw a party! Invite everyone you know. Invite Dolly. Just like MJTJ. Wish I could come. I miss you.

Now Dini's feet are tap-tap-tapping. Her brain is buzz-buzz-buzzing. She can't stand it. She has to talk to Maddie.

"Can I call Maddie on your phone?" she asks Dad.

"Wait just a minute," he says, "we can do better than that."

"How?" Dini is puzzled. What is Dad going to do? Is he going to take Dini back to Maryland this minute?

No, he is not. "Here's a high-tech solution," says Dad. "I've been working on this for a while. Internet-video call."

"Wow," Dini says.

Dad explains, "We thought it would be nice if you girls could talk to each other this way."

"No kidding," Dini says. "You set that all up?"

"That's right," Dad says, double-clicking away on his machine. "You two peas in a pod, bugs in a rug. You and your pal Maddie. What do you think?" He is practically dancing with delight himself as he pulls down the menu and click-click-clicks.

The computer *brrrrrrings* like a telephone. Then, "There's Maddie!" Dini yells.

"Dini!" Maddie says. Her voice breaks up a little, and so does her picture, coming and going in small waves of color, but who cares?

"Oh, Daddy," Dini says, "you are a genius."

"Takes one to know one," says Dad.

Chapter Thirty-one

Help

THE LAST TIME DINI looked at the clock, it was two in the morning. Now it is five. Dini has gone over the details of her party over and over in her mind, and it has kept her wide awake. She has decided on a date for the party—this coming Sunday. Mom and Dad said okay.

Now for the invitations, what filmi people call behind-the-scenes work. In their ten-minute computer video phone call, Dini and Maddie have managed to nail all the off-camera stuff it will take to pull off this creative project.

Since Dini can't sleep anyway, she gets up and starts working on the invitations. She opened up a file the night before and typed one up and printed out copies. Now she writes a list of all the people she knows, and addresses an envelope to each one in her tidiest handwriting. Veeran and his wife and baby, c/o Swapnagiri Clinic. Mr. Mani of Dreamy-cakes Bakery.

And yes, Priya and her uncle. They are part of the plot fix whether or not they want to be, and Dini cannot afford to give up on them yet. Sampy the watchman. And of course there is one last envelope with only a name on it because Dini has not yet found that person, does not know her address.

She folds and folds again. She puts the invitations in the envelopes. She licks the envelopes closed. She finds stamps in the kitchen drawer where Dad keeps the stamps. She sticks them on all the envelopes that need stamps, which is all of them except the one for Sampy. This is a big job.

Oh, why is it that she always ends up having to send Dolly letters with incomplete addresses? Maybe they'll know at the post office. It'll work out. Somehow. It has to.

But when Dini finally goes downstairs clutching the bundle of party invitations in her hand, she finds another whole drama unfolding. Sampy is showing in two men who are lugging a red metal cylinder. They half lift, half roll it across the floor and right into Dini's path.

"Yikes!" says Dini as the top of the cylinder tilts her way. The men grab at it. They catch it just in time. Narrow escape. That cylinder could flatten a person.

Mom is clutching at the wall. Dad is clutching the sofa he sits on. The invitations are all over the floor.

"Mind-mind-mind," Sampy warns everyone.

"What's all that?" Mom says as Dini gathers up her invitations.

Dini starts to explain, but in this scene, Mom is no longer waiting for an answer. The camera has shifted and is now on the cylinder, which is being half rolled, half carried into the kitchen.

"Watch out" and "Be careful," say Mom and Dad together as the bottom of the cylinder grazes the door.

The cylinder delivery men ignore them all.

Sampy clears his throat and steps into the fray. "Left, left," says Sampy.

The men shuffle left.

"Now right," says Sampy. "Now more right."

Shuffle-shuffle. Left-left, right-right. This is practically a dance. A little music, a few swirling rainbows, and—

"More, more," Sampy commands. "Now go. Careful, this is not a warehouse where you can throw things around."

Dini can see that when Sampy takes charge of something, he gets it done. That is one useful skill. Perhaps it is no coincidence that Sampy is here. Perhaps he has a role in this unfolding story.

"Finally," Dini says, skipping out of the way, "we can eat food that's not burned."

The delivery guys take a long time to set the cylinder up and to attach it to the stove. Then they hang around expectantly.

Mom gives them each a couple of rupees. They hang around some more, discussing the weight of empty versus full gas cylinders. Then they finally take off.

Sampy sniffs. "They are from the plains," he says by way of explanation. "Greedy people, these plains people. Probably waiting for you to give them a cup of coffee. And then what? Lunch they will expect, then tea, is it?" He snorts at the nerve of those cylinder delivery guys. Then he opens the door and exits with a final glare.

"I'll be right back," Dini tells her parents, who

anyway are busy admiring the cylinder. And she follows Sampy out.

Who knew that Sampy could take charge like this? Dini sees that she has to turn this man from a bystander into an ally in the Finding Dolly project. It takes a sharp eye to recognize a potential ally, and Dini is suddenly feeling sharp-eyed.

Chapter Thirty-two

Dropping of Jaws

SUNNY VILLA ESTATES has a system for residents who want to post letters but don't feel like going all the way to the post office. The system is a basket that sits by Sampy's gate. If you have a letter to mail, you simply go drop it in the basket. Then the next time Sampy goes to town, he puts the letters in a bag and takes them to the post office for you.

By the time Dini catches up with Sampy, he has gone back to sitting by the side of the road and chewing on a bit of grass. He gives Dini a friendly glower.

"Will you take these out today?" she asks him politely. And now she can see it is just his eyebrows that make him look mad all the time. It is because they join in the middle, becoming one eyebrow. It's not anything to do with who he is. Amazing, the things you can figure out when you bother to listen-listen, look-look.

Sampy looks up at the sky. He looks at the tea-gardens and the far horizon. "Maybe," he says, "if there is time. Otherwise tomorrow."

Dini explains that they are invitations to a party. "If they go out today, will they get to everyone by tomorrow?" she asks.

"Hmm . . . maybe," says Sampy. "Party, is it?"

Dini gives him the envelope without a stamp. "This one's for you."

Sampy looks at her as if she has suddenly sprouted wings and is chirping like one of those green birds in the trees. He takes a deep breath. "Me?" he says. "Where does it say that?"

Dini points to his name on the envelope. "Oh," he says. "Yes, that is my name." He is quite excited by seeing his name on the envelope.

"Yes, yes," he says. He picks up a stick and writes his name in the dirt. He writes like someone who is not used to writing. "A party?" he says thoughtfully. Maybe he is also someone who is not used to being invited to parties.

"Yes," Dini says. "Will you come?"

Sampy considers the offer. "Certainly," he says, "unless, of course, something urgent comes up on that day."

"And you'll take the others to the post office?"

Sampy nods his head, side to side. "Why put it off?" he says. "I'll take them right now. All local, right?"

"Yes," Dini says.

"No problem. They'll get there tomorrow." He waves his hands in a kind of curving movement, and for some reason this makes Dini feel very sure that he is right. They will get there on time. No question. Sampy's on her side.

Dini nods back eagerly to seal the deal.

But Sampy is not done. He's looking at the envelopes with great interest. "Who all will be coming to this very important gathering?" he wants to know.

Dini reads the names out to him. When she gets to the last one, without a proper address, she hesitates.

Sampy chews on his grass stalk. He seems fascinated by the letters marching across each envelope. "I can write my name in Tamil and in English," he confesses, "but that is all I know how to write. Someday I would like to write like that. Very beautiful."

"Thank you," says Dini, who has not thought of cursive writing as an especially important skill, not since second grade, but it is clearly a big deal for Sampy. "I can show you how, if you like."

Sampy's muscles twitch. That is possibly a smile, but Dini is not sure. He waves his grass stalk at the envelopes. "Who is that last one? Read that out for me also."

"It's Dolly Singh," Dini admits. "I don't have an address for her. I know she's here somewhere. Do you think they'll know at the post office?" She wonders if Sampy knows who Dolly Singh is, so she adds, "Dolly Singh the movie star. I really want her to come."

Sampy says, "You will really teach me how to write like that?"

"Sure," Dini says. She pulls out her green stripy notebook that is always in her pocket. She shows him the pages she has filled up. "Look. It's not hard."

And that is when Sampy drops his bombshell.

He gets up. He stretches. "I know where is Miss Dolly Singh," he says. "Many messages I have taken to her from cottage number one in the past month. Many-many, and return messages also, even some back and forth by Speed Post. Very sad story."

Cottage number I. That's Chickoo Uncle's house.

"I will deliver this one," Sampy says. "Personally. Have you seen her newest fillum?"

"MJTJ!" Dini says. "Of course. It's brilliant."

"But so sad," says Sampy. "Not even one happy song."

Dini has heard of people's jaws being described as dropping out of sheer shock or amazement. Dad, in fact, counts this dropping of jaws in his collection of nifty expressions that he uses with great glee from time to time. Dini has never actually seen anyone's jaw drop. But as Sampy picks up the letters, steadies his old bicycle that's leaning against the gate, gets on it, and wobbles off on his important errand, she finds that is exactly what has happened to her jaw.

She was right! Something sad was going on in Dolly's life when she made that movie! It's a wonderful thing when a true fan finds another who shares her views.

Chapter Thirty-three

Throwing a Party

THE TABLES GROAN under their load of curry puffs, chocolate cake, and other delectable edibles. The day is fine. The sky is blue. The silver and green ribbons that Dini threaded through the branches of the bottlebrush tree look fabulously dreamy swaying and lifting in the gentle breeze.

It seems all the invitations arrived at their destinations in a timely manner. Veeran is here, and his wife, Mala, and their baby, who is wearing tiny gold baby-size earrings and blinking at everybody.

"Hello, Miss Nandini," Veeran says.

"Vanakkam," says his wife in Tamil. Here in Swapnagiri, just by listen-listening to people around her, Dini is learning a third language, after Hindi and English. Maybe someday she will travel to lots of places like Priya's parents and learn all those languages too. Filmi people are like that, always wanting to explore different settings.

"Eeee-goo-goo," says the baby, who speaks her own language. She grabs Dini's finger and cackles. Babies are odd little people, Dini thinks. Just having your finger grabbed by one is enough to make a person laugh.

Priya arrives with her uncle, followed by a tall, skinny lady with a whispery voice. She's the one who was out working in her garden on the day that Dini first met Priya. Her name is Sita Chellappa and she lives in cottage number 4. Her sausage dog is here with her; his name is Inji.

"Means 'Ginger,'" says Priya, who is speaking to Dini now, but only two words at a time.

"I Know," Dini says, trying to capitalize. But Priya has not heard. Priya is following a bird into the branches of a bottlebrush tree, puzzling it with her pitch-perfect calls.

"Why all the filmi decorations?" Mrs. Chellappa whispers.

"Our daughter's work," Mom explains.

"Young people," says Mrs. Chellappa in a tone that indicates she much prefers dogs.

Chickoo Uncle praises the garden of cottage

number 6. "Excellent," he says to Mom and Dad. "Look at all these beautiful flowers."

"That is my wife's doing," Dad says. Mom smiles. She has been digging in the dirt in her spare time, and surreptitiously singing to the canna plants in the hope that they will bloom big and bright, red and yellow. She will deny that this is what she does, of course, but Dini has caught her in the act more than once.

Mrs. Chellappa inquires after their gas cylinder, which seems to indicate that everyone in Sunny Villa Estates knows about the comings and goings and doings of everyone else. Dini leaves them chatting about the difficulty of getting those things into a house where the driveway is uphill rather than downhill.

Forget the gas cylinder—it's doing fine inside the kitchen. Forget Priya's frowny face—that can change later on. With all the cheeping and the buzz of conversation and the glossy green hillsides, the whole world feels alive and practically dancing in anticipation. But where is Dolly?

Sampy said he will stand by the outside gate and alert Dini when the guest of honor comes. So of course Dini keeps circling to the edge of the garden and looking down the red dirt road to make sure she doesn't miss the grand appearance. What is the point of even going to a movie if you miss the grand appearance of the star herself?

Circle-circle. Listen-listen, look-look. It will all work out fine. It does in MJTJ, after all.

One . . . two . . . three . . . now! Sampy waves both his arms in the air.

Dini rushes to the inside gate of cottage number 6 and throws it open.

And there she is, Dolly Singh herself, getting out of a taxi. She is in a parrot green sari with sequins along the edges. On her feet she has silver strappy sandals, which are not exactly making it easy for her to walk along the red dirt road of Sunny Villa Estates, but she is bravely elegant in them nonetheless.

She is so small.

Dolly Singh

is so

small.

Why, Dini is almost as tall as she is. Wait till Dini tells Maddie this.

Without even knowing it, Dini has been expecting someone taller. Of course, real people's faces do not float on screens, so it was probably not fair to expect Dolly to show up that way. Still, it's a little—just a little—disappointing. That's what it is.

But then Dolly sweeps through the gate, and Dini can see that height is not everything. Presence is what counts.

Dolly speaks. "Hello," she says, "you must be Dini." It is not much, but Dini nearly faints with delight. She finds herself babbling about the letter she sent Dolly from Maryland and how dizzy with joy she was to get a reply.

"A true fan," says Dolly, waving her arms in the air for emphasis. A dangly silver earring falls from her ear to the ground. She stoops to pick it up.

Dini gets there before Dolly does and they bump heads—*clunk!*—on the way up. "Oh!" Dini cries. "I'm sorry!" This is not how she's planned her very first meeting with Dolly Singh.

In MJTJ when the heroine (that is to say, Dolly) brings together all the people who have had disagreements throughout the fillum, they see one another and burst out crying. Not with grief, but because they are touched by her doing this very wonderful thing for them.

They hug. They make up. They are all grateful to her for fixing their lives.

This does not happen at Dini's party.

Instead, this is what happens: Dini leads Dolly to the food table, where Dolly meets Mr. Mani. Dolly is charming, naturally. Mr. Mani is charmed. Naturally.

Dini introduces Dolly to Dad, then Mom. They are polite, although Dini suspects it will take more than charm to impress them.

Mr. Mani offers Dolly a plate with a curry puff and a slice of chocolate cake on it. "Oh, I adore chocolate cake," says Dolly.

That is when it happens. Someone else, hearing Dolly's voice, turns. Who would not turn at hearing Dolly's fabulous voice? That is no surprise.

The someone who turns is Chickoo Uncle.

This is Dini's moment.

She is about to say, "It's a matter of love," which is the cue in MJTJ for the great reconciliation to begin, with all the tears and hugging that go with it. She has even practiced the line in Hindi: "Pyaar ki baat hai."

But before she can utter it, Dolly says, "Oh no!" She is looking right at Chickoo Uncle. "I can't . . . oh no!" She waves her arms.

The plate drops. The curry puff and chocolate cake land in the grass.

Mr. Mani utters a cry of horror.

Chickoo Uncle looks as if he is about to burst into tears. Or song. Song would be better. "Only Clear Skies Will Cure a Broken Heart." That would do nicely.

But in this scene that has crept into a kind of nasty slow motion for all the wrong reasons, Chickoo Uncle does not sing.

Instead, Inji the little sausage dog, who does not even have a role, jumps out of Mrs. Chellappa's arms and begins stuffing his little doggy face with chocolate cake.

Mrs. Chellappa runs to grab him. She trips Dolly up. It is not quite the trip-up that the villainous pair, Sukha and Dukha, manage to accomplish in MJTJ, but for a person untrained in stunt maneuvers, it is close.

Some people may call it coincidence that Inji, Mrs. Chellappa, and Dolly all manage to be in the same spot at the same time, so that there is a collision. Some coincidences can be like that. Purely unpleasant, and is that also kismet?

Dolly screams.

Dolly can really scream.

"Now you've Done it," says Priya. That is more than two words, but they are the wrong words.

"Good Job" was what the script called for.

Dolly's scream sails out into the tea-gardens. It zings across the valley and bounces off the opposite mountain, so that it seems to become several screa-ea-ea-ea-eams, each with its own set of echoing mini screams.

Dolly runs for the gate. "Where *is* that taxi?" she demands.

The taxi driver, who has been enjoying the day by chatting with Sampy over a curry puff, snaps to attention.

"Wait!" Dini cries. "Please. I need to tell you something." This is not in any script, but she doesn't care.

On account of this messed-up cast who will not

do what they are supposed to do, Dini has been unable to show Dolly her green stripy notebook. She has not even been able to tell Dolly the most important thing there is to tell her—that Dolly's first movie came out the day that she, Dini, was born! All the time she has had to worry about frowny girls and flying plates of delectable snacks, and silly yappy dogs.

Bakvaas, that's all it is. Just a foolish dream she had, that one day she would meet Dolly and they would be friends and she would call Maddie . . . and . . . and . . . and . . . It all caves in like a chocolate cake that a monkey got its paws into.

Dolly gets into the taxi. Before you can say "Take two," she is gone.

And that is not all. Priya says to Dini, "How could you Invite Her? You are Crazy. And you know what Else? She is Crazy. Do you know what she Did?" Which is a lot of words, but that is no comfort.

"What?" Dini is feeling whiny by now, and that is not in the script either, but who cares.

Priya makes the long, low noises of wedding music. "She Promised my uncle she would Marry him," she spits out.

"*Marry?*" says Dini.

Priya nods grimly. "He said she could even shoot her next Film right here. She was even going to call the movie *Sunny Villa*."

Dini stares at Priya.

"My mother says Chickoo Uncle is the Sensitive Type," Priya says. "She was really Mean to him. Do you know what she called him?"

"What?" Dini whispers.

Priya brings her face close to Dini's. She says, "She really hurt his Feelings. She called him a Potato Nose."

And so for the second time in a week Dini's jaw drops.

Chapter Thirty-four

Meh!

A GOATHERD WITH DREAMS of moving up in the world is driving his precious animals along the red dirt roads of Sunny Villa Estates when something makes him stop so suddenly that for a split second he thinks he is revisiting an old, familiar nightmare.

It is a scream.

Again? That scream? That ghostly, disembodied scream is everywhere!

"Meh," go the goats. "Meh-eh-eh! Meh-eh-eh!" The dreamy goatherd's goats scatter up and down the hillside, which is what goats do when they are distraught.

The dream is replaced by a terrible thing that clutches at the goatherd. Fear.

This scream will undoubtedly give these goats indigestion. Their milk will be sour. It will curdle.

It may even be bitter. And then what will happen to the goatherd's dream of moving up to a cow and selling the milk and buying some chickens and selling the eggs to the Dreamycakes Bakery?

Now instead of dreaming this fine dream, he has to run up and down rows of tea bushes, in between kurinji plants and bottlebrush trees and even some thorny shrubs that leave unpleasant, itchy scratches on his arms and legs. He has to gather his darling goats.

"Come on, my little jackfruits," he coos to them. "Come along, my little oranges, my beautiful custard apples! Let's find some other grazing place, far from this ghoulish presence."

As fast as he can, the goatherd rounds up his panicked animals and scurries away from the source of this hideously terrifying scream.

Chapter Thirty-five

Worse

"WHAT AM I DOING HERE?" says Priya's uncle Chickoo.

"You are drinking tea," Dini tells him.

Priya's uncle showed up unexpectedly and very early this morning, the morning after the no-good, terrible bakvaas party. Ever since Mom invited him in, he has been guzzling cups of tea in the living room of cottage number 6 and looking miserable.

"I'm sorry," Dini says, and she doesn't say it only because her parents are glaring at her, even though they most certainly are. It *was* her fault. She is drooping inside like a canna plant that someone has forgotten to water.

Chickoo Dev is gracious, and he makes mild noises pooh-poohing her apology. "No, no," he says. "It's okay."

Mom and Dad disagree. They think Dini has

been meddling in things that are none of her business, and they have said so already in as many ways as they can.

"What is to be done?" Mr. Chickoo Dev says. "I mean about . . . you know, the bigger picture. Sometimes I feel quite out of my depth."

What does he mean by that? What bigger picture? For one moment Dini wonders if he is talking about a movie.

"There is my sister and her husband in America," says Mr. Chickoo Dev, "on their way to Haiti—or is it Chile? I forget—in a matter of weeks, and here I am." He takes another moody sip.

"Have a biscuit," Mom says. She offers a plate of those cookies, the rose petal kind, from Dreamycakes.

Chickoo Dev refuses with a small shudder. Perhaps it is just the memory of the Dreamycakes curry puff and cake falling to the ground. "I've had cats and dogs before," he says, "but pets don't throw tantrums. They don't refuse to cooperate." He throws up his hands, all helpless. Dini begins to feel sorry for him. Nobody knows as well as she does what it's like when things do not go your way, even when you have done everything you could possibly do.

Mom says, "They're more work than pets, that's for sure," and she's smiling fondly—about what, Dini has no idea.

"Kids, she means," Dad says. He rumples Dini's hair. Dini wishes he wouldn't. But timing is everything, and even she, who messed up so badly on her own timing the day before, can see that now is not the moment to tell Dad to quit ruffling her hair.

"You have to feed them, send them to school," says Mr. Chickoo Dev. "Make sure they become responsible people who can take their place in the world."

"Who are you talking about?" Dini says. Her parents are shaking their heads at her, but she can't stand being in the dark like this.

Mr. Chickoo Dev sips his tea, then clears his throat. "My niece, Priya," he says, as if that was perfectly obvious.

"Oh." Dini wishes she hadn't asked. She wishes they'd go back to talking about the euro-dollar exchange rate like they used to do, and leave her out of it.

She tries to make a noise like a train whistle, like Priya does, but she can't. Her mouth is not shaped right or she doesn't know what to do with her teeth or something.

"Sweetoo, don't spit," says Mom in the voice of an adult who is going to get grumpy in a minute.

"I'm not," Dini starts to say, and loses the bite of cookie that she has just taken, which is of course called a biscuit here in India but never mind she loses it anyway. They all look at her, even Mr. Chickoo Dev.

It is too bad that they can't just do this all over. Retakes are a good thing, but life doesn't let you save the bloopers for the archives and try that scene again.

Mr. Chickoo Dev says, "Priya is a very shy and sensitive girl."

Dini thinks, Me too. I am sensitive. Maybe not so shy, but sensitive. Doesn't anyone care about that?

"That's what I said to Mrs. Balu," Chickoo Uncle says. "I can use some support in looking after her while her parents are not here, I said." He seems to be plunging deeper into gloom with each word.

Mom and Dad murmur their sympathy.

"And she's impulsive," Mr. Chickoo Dev says, as if he is speaking about a rare flower. "Once a person like that has made up her mind . . ." Sad little sounds issue from his mouth, which makes Dini wonder if Priya's talent runs in the family. "Now she has decided she doesn't want to stay here anymore. She wants to go join her parents in Washington, D.C."

"She does?" says Dini.

Chickoo Dev nods sadly. "This is of course impossible. You probably know the United States government isn't going to let any kid into the country just because she wants to go." He complains that Priya refuses to understand that sending a kid is not as simple a thing as mailing a letter. "She's sitting on the roof of cottage number one," he says, "just sitting and sitting. She won't come down."

Dini is thinking that she might like to be up on a roof by herself just like Priya right now, although maybe not the same roof, when the phone rings from its place on the dining-room wall.

"I'll get it," Dini says, and escapes around the corner.

It is Maddie. "I tried to do that computer calling thing," she says, "but it's late right now and I don't know how. So, did you find her? Did you get them back together? Is she going to make a new movie?"

"No!" Dini wails. "It's all a big mess, Maddie, you wouldn't believe it."

"I'm so sorry, Dini," Maddie says.

"No," Dini wails again. She is feeling very waily just now and she does not like it one bit. She is not used to feeling this way.

She tells Maddie about Priya and Chickoo Uncle and the noise in the car and Dolly screaming when she saw Chickoo Uncle, which must mean she hates him! That's the exact opposite of love, the plot point Dini was after.

She's not sure how much of it Maddie gets because, truthfully, even while she's telling the story, it all seems like such a big jumble. Somehow, in Swapnagiri everything gets tied up with everything else; it is just that kind of a place. How could Maddie possibly understand what Mr. Chickoo Dev would call the bigger picture?

"Dini," Maddie says. "Can I ask you something?"

"Why not?" says Dini sadly.

"Would you be mad if . . . what I mean to say is, if I told you . . . how would you feel . . ."

What is Maddie trying to say? "Just slow down

and say it, Maddie," Dini tells her. "Tell you what—it can't be worse than anything that's happened here."

Maddie says very fast, "I made a new friend and she invited me to her house. For a sleepover."

That stops Dini.

Maddie says, "She's new in my neighborhood. Her name is Brenna. She's nice. I think you'd like her."

There was a time when the idea of Maddie making a new friend—a sleepover kind of friend, at that—would have been yikes and eek, maybe even aargh and blech.

But now Dini thinks, Well, it's not in the jaw-dropping category, a sleepover. So what? If Priya would get off that roof, Dini could maybe invite her for one.

Maddie is still talking. "So what do you think? Mom says I should take her cell phone along so you can call me if something—you know—comes up."

"Something . . . ?" Dini repeats because she has no idea what Maddie is talking about.

"Something Dolly," Maddie explains.

"Oh. Yeah. I mean, sure you should go. Really, Maddie."

"Really?" says Maddie.

"Really," says Dini. "Really and Absolutely, and don't Worry, I'll call you if Anything comes up." With a small shock she sees that not only is this true, but she's speaking in capital letters.

"Are you going to keep trying?" Maddie says. "To get Dolly and that Chickoo guy to make up?"

"I don't know," Dini says. It makes her sad to admit it, even to herself, but she is a little disappointed—in Dolly. That was an incredible scream. There is no question. No one can scream like Dolly.

"You have to, Dini," Maddie says. "No one else can."

"I just wish she hadn't screamed," Dini says. "You know what I mean?"

"I know," Maddie says.

Somehow just those little words from Maddie— "I know"—set the world right side up again by the time Dini says good-bye and hangs up. Maddie knows how Dini feels.

Sometimes a small comfort like that is all that you need. Dini goes to her room and curls up with the latest issue of *Filmi Kumpnee*.

Leafing through the pages of the latest *Filmi*

Kumpnee magazine only adds a sprinkle of red chili powder to the curry puff of Dini's puzzlement.

> Dolly Singh fans, we are sad to report that one of our hardworking *Filmi Kumpnee* reporters was savagely attacked. The regrettable incident took place outside the residence of Mr. Soli Dustup, who rules over Starlite Studios with an iron fist.
>
> When we tried to get a word with him, just one word—"Is it love?" we asked. "And if so, tragic or joyful?"—that was when the attack occurred.
>
> Ironically, the weapon was a rolled-up copy of your favorite magazine. Yes, life is unfair and unjust. We were brutally attacked with our own *Filmi Kumpnee* magazine.
>
> And so for the first time in many issues we are so sorry to say that we have no word on Dolly.
>
> But stay alert. We will too. And we'll be back.

Chapter Thirty-six

Finding Roses

SOLI DUSTUP OF STARLITE STUDIOS, Mumbai (used to be called Bombay), has had a bad day. His plane was late, so he missed the mountain train and only just managed to get a ride up to Swapnagiri in a white Qualis.

The Qualis, which was full of medical supplies, was driven by a complete madman who insisted on driving at three times the speed limit all the way, paying no attention to useful signs like IF YOU DASH, YOU WILL CRASH and ARRIVE ALIVE. By way of explanation, all that this crazy driver would say was that it was Tuesday and he had to get those supplies to a clinic for the patients. "You lunatic," Mr. Dustup wanted to tell him, "you save your own life first and mine, then worry about those patients." But he couldn't say a word; he was too busy closing his eyes so that the road didn't speed past him at such a terrifying tempo.

Several times Mr. Dustup came close to demanding that the maniac just let him get off on the side of the road. Only the thought of having to walk all the way up the mountain stopped him. Some people would not, of course, find that prospect daunting, but Mr. Soli Dustup is not one of those health fiends. He is not overly fond of exercise. The clean mountain air does not call to him as it does to so many people who come to Swapnagiri seeking it.

What is calling to Mr. Soli Dustup is his work, his life, the movie business he loves, and the rupees that it makes for Starlite Studios. And in order to make those rupees—preferably lots of them—he needs Dolly back. He has tried to call her a hundred times, but her phone rings and rings and no one answers it.

Does she even know what hard work it was to send out those hundreds and hundreds of "Dearest Friend and Fan" letters on her behalf?

He has even tried to resign himself to the prospect of no Dolly. He has tried out a dozen different female leads for the next movie project, but it's no use. All of them are flops. Worst of all, he has had to fend off (practically with his bare hands) a dreadfully nosy reporter from *Filmi Kumpnee* magazine.

Soli needs Dolly back, but more, Starlite Studios needs her. The fillum world needs her.

That is why Soli is now trudging up and down this very steep street trying to find a florist in Swapnagiri. He has the vague idea that taking Dolly a dozen roses may help to win her back. Maybe, he thinks, they can come to some agreement. Maybe he will say, "If you just take back that nasty name you called me—Jug-Handle-Ears . . ."

But no, he thinks with a sigh, Dolly is not the kind of person to reconsider a thing like that.

Dolly is a difficult person. A temperamental person. But then, he thinks, of course she is. She is an artist. In his mind he even adds an *e* to the word, which is what movie types do when they want to show that their work is sensitive and important at the same time. There is no question, Soli thinks distractedly. An artiste is what Dolly is.

Finding roses is proving harder than Soli thought. It is not that there are no roses in this town. There are lots of roses. Red, yellow, pink, they are in full flower. They are bursting out of people's gardens.

They are budding on canes in parks marked NO SPITTING. NO BLASTING LOUD MUSIC INTO PEACEFUL GARDEN. ABSOLUTELY NO FLOUR PICKING.

Soli Dustup is a fussy reader. It annoys him greatly that the painter of this sign thinks he is talking about a bakery and not a garden. Soli debates picking a dozen roses from this place and pleading superior spelling when he is caught, which he will be, because right there is a policeman walking up and down and wearing a stern look. "I was not taking any flour," Mr. Soli Dustup can see himself bravely protesting. "If these people want their local laws to be obeyed, they should learn how to spell."

But he is a practical man, Mr. Dustup, and courting arrest is not what he has come to this silly town to do.

Here is the thing. Soli has walked up and down Blue Mountain Road, the main street in Swapnagiri, until two blisters (one on his right heel and one under his left big toe) have begun sending small, screaming signals to his nerve endings. And in all this walking he has not spotted a single shop where he can buy even one measly blossom.

People come to Swapnagiri for a restful vacation,

or because they always wanted to work in the clinic and somebody is now paying them to do so. Sometimes they come because they have lost their way while trying to go somewhere else in this part of India. Or else they come to grow tea. They do not come to buy fancy bouquets. Soli is finding out that long-stemmed roses are not a concept known to the business people of Swapnagiri.

"Roses?" says the cloth-shop lady when Soli knocks on her door. "Sorry, I don't need any roses."

Soli tries to tell her he wants to buy, not sell, roses. He points to the bush of yellow roses in a pot outside her shop. Yellow is not Dolly's favorite color, but Soli is desperate.

"You want to cut my roses?" the lady says, brandishing a large pair of shears and missing Soli's ear by inches.

Such a thought, Soli swears, backing away, was never in his mind.

Out on the road he looks around. Then he spies an oasis in this tomfool, madcap place. It is a bakery. He decides to go there. If roses are not to be had, then that chocolate fudge in the window will do. Dolly is mad about chocolate.

Chapter Thirty-seven

Early Retirement

"SPEED POST TO SEND A LETTER from one end of this town to another?" Ramanna the Swapnagiri postal carrier has to sit down, so taken aback is he at this extravagance. "And how many letters, I ask you? Back and forth, back and forth." He shakes his head. "I do not think my heart can stand it."

"What do you mean?" says the postmaster. "It's only a few more letters than usual."

True, the mail between Sunny Villa Estates cottage number one and the guesthouse of the Blue Mountain School has been keeping Ramanna busier than usual. True, he had to make three extra trips just to handle it. Speed Post means expedited delivery—India Post is clear about that. And the Swapnagiri postmaster has only one letter carrier to rely on. Not since it was founded in the days before Indian independence has this post office ever handled so many speedy letters all needing to get there in superfast time.

"What do they think I am, a blasted whirling dervish?" says Ramanna.

"It *is* your job to deliver the letters," the postmaster protests.

Ramanna thinks. He counts on his fingers the number of years of service he has put in. He does not have enough fingers. He could retire today. He could. Then he would not have to run around at the bidding of every fool person who decides to dash off a letter by Speed Post on a whim.

"I have made up my mind," he says to the postmaster. "I am taking early retirement. I will write you a letter to that effect. Naturally, I will not be sending it by Speed Post."

"Oh dear, oh dear," murmurs the postmaster. Life is very unfair, he thinks, always making more work for people who already have enough.

Chapter Thirty-eight

Getting a Grip

THE DAY AFTER CHICKOO UNCLE'S visit Mom is humming her way through her morning coffee. "What is that tune?" she says. "I can't get it out of my head."

"Mom," Dini says, "that's a Dolly song. 'Sunno-sunno! Dekho-dekho!'" Mom is humming a Dolly song? If that is not a miracle, Dini does not know what is.

"Is it? I've probably heard you playing it over and over," Mom says. "How are you today, darling?" She gives Dini an anxious look, no doubt worrying about her because she thinks Dini is having a hard time and behaving oddly as a result.

But Dini is willing to let bygones be bygones. Right now she is seeing the big picture, although maybe not quite the one Chickoo Uncle was talking about. "I'm fine," she says.

And she is. Seeing the big picture has that effect. Dini is not only fine, she is ready to start listen-listening, look-looking, all over again. Reading that *Filmi Kumpnee* article helped her to make up her mind. She is so ahead of them. She can't give up.

And here before her she sees Mom. A parent, sure, with many of the faults that come with that job description. But also an example of not giv-ing up. "Mom," Dini says, handing her mother the bag and lunch she will surely need, "did you really apply for this job six times before they gave it to you? Six times?" It does seem like a lot. She opens the door for Mom.

"I had to write a grant," Mom says. "And yes, it got turned down five times before they gave it to me. Why?"

"Just asking."

Then Mom hugs Dini, and hurries down the red dirt road toward the bus stop. Dini watches from the front step until Mom has rounded the bend and disappeared. She goes back inside the little house with the blinky shutters, and she is think-ing hard.

In her movies Dolly is often beautiful and

charming and witty and all the things you would expect of a fine and proper star. But when the time comes to do something, there is also no doer like Dolly. Didn't she throw the villain off the pier in MJTJ, making him swim a dozen shivery miles home? Didn't she haul in a whole fishing boat of smugglers just two scenes later and show the hero that she was on his side when he thought she wasn't?

It is, of course, more difficult to be a doer in your own life than in the movies, where a whole boatload of scriptwriters, makeup people, costume and set-design and location people, not to mention special-effects people and body doubles and whatnot, are there to help you. Even that person who is rather peculiarly called a grip, and who is perhaps there to help the star get one when she needs to.

This is why Dolly undoubtedly needs help—and she will get it. Maddie is right. No one can do this but Dini because no one else gets the big picture.

Dini must keep trying. If Mom can write that grant over and over, and be turned down five times before she got it, Dini can get this story line to where it needs to go.

But someone else needs to get a grip now, and Dini has to go take care of that first. She tells Dad, "I'm going to Priya's house, okay?"

"Oh?" Dad says, pushing his chair back. "Mending broken fences, are you?"

Dini can see if she hangs around, he may look up at the crack in the ceiling, and then she'll be stuck for goodness knows how long. "Daddy, later. I don't have time right now."

"All right, you busy person," he says. "Stay inside—"

"I know, the main gate," Dini finishes for him, and she's already running to the road. Soon she is turning into the driveway of Sunny Villa cottage number 1, which is bigger than a couple of the other cottages, at least, put together.

When Dini knocks, Veeran's wife, Mala, opens the door. It turns out she sweeps and mops the floor in cottage number 1 and sometimes also cooks dinner, because left to himself, Mr. Chickoo Dev would be useless at such things.

Mala waves Dini in and says she'll go get Priya. Then she grins at Dini, tucks her sari up, and walks off to the kitchen, with her toe rings on her bare feet going *clink-clink* on the shiny polished tile floor. Dini thinks it must be fun to wear toe rings like that, going *clink-clink* on things when you walk.

"I thought I'd find you on the roof," Dini says when Priya shows up.

"I couldn't stay there all Night," Priya says. "Even if I Wanted to."

And that is when Dini sees that it is not Priya who needs to get a grip, it is Dini herself. All the time she's been chasing after Dolly, here was a person who could be her friend, and Dini has not even given her the time of day. Which is a Dad way of saying she hasn't paid her any attention and now she is so very sorry about that.

"Priya, I don't want you to go to Washington, D.C.," Dini says, and she means every word.

"You Don't?" Priya's face has surprise all over it. "Why?"

Dini swallows. "Priya," she says, "I'm Sorry about that Party, and I want to be Friends." She thinks she's getting the uppercase, even if she can't do the sound effects.

"Well, if you put it like That," Priya says, and

chirps like the green birds that hang upside down from the bottlebrush flowers.

And so they talk. They talk about Bombay and Washington, D.C., about the Gateway of India and the Washington Monument, around both of which you can find—what a coincidence!—pigeons. They talk about this Blue Mountain School, which seems quite nice, but it will be strange to be new there.

Priya says, "Want to take the Bus into town with me? I have to post some Letters, and Sampy took the basket Out already."

"Sure," says Dini, "but I need to call my dad first."

Priya makes a sound like a ringing phone, and hands Dini a cordless.

Dad seems pleased and surprised. "To town, by bus?" he says. "With your friend Priya?"

"Uh-huh," Dini says cautiously.

"So she's your friend again?" Dad says.

"Uh-huh." She hopes this won't take too long, but she is prepared to keep saying "Uh-huh" if she must.

"Be careful crossing the road," he tells her.

"Uh-huh!" says Dini, greatly relieved.

On the bus, going past the tea-gardens and then the shops and houses, she talks to Priya about a hundred things, but not about Dolly and Chickoo Uncle. Not yet.

Chapter Thirty-nine

Pepper

WHEN LAL THE POSTMAN and his new wife, Lila, get off the mountain train at Swapnagiri Station on a Tuesday morning, they are at once enchanted by the beauty of the place.

"Such scenery . . . ," says Lal.

"And such fine air," says his wife.

"A person could ride a bicycle for miles here . . . ," says Lal.

"And not even be out of breath," says his wife.

Being newly married and all, they are delighted to be able to complete each other's sentences.

They drop their modest bags off at the tiny hotel (called the Open Arms, as in "We Welcome You With") where they have made a reservation all the way from far-off Mumbai. The Open Arms is right behind a tea and spices shop run by the husband of the woman who owns the hotel. Lal and Lila pop in at the shop to take a look and meet some of the locals.

"Chai masala . . . ," Lal marvels.

"So many kinds," adds Lila.

The tea-and-spices man is pleased at their interest. Indeed, he has several varieties of tea spice—some heavier on pepper, others on cardamom, others running more to ginger, or cinnamon and cloves. "Also, we have some very fine freshly ground pepper," he says. "Would you like to buy some?"

Lal is about to say, "No, thank you," but his wife says, "Fresh pepper? Oh, we should take some back to your mother in Mumbai." So they buy a small bag. Even if it makes them sneeze a little, they agree that it is very fine pepper.

Bidding good-bye to the tea-and-spices man, Lal and Lila proceed up Blue Mountain Road. Soon they arrive at the Dreamycakes Bakery.

"Oh look!" says Lila.

"Oh no!" says Lal.

An unexpected customer has arrived at the bakery before them. The customer has two beady eyes, little grasping hands, and a tail. And it is terrorizing the owner of the bakery. Years after the last unfortunate time that this happened, a monkey has once again found its way into Dreamycakes Bakery.

"Help!" yells Mr. Mani. "Help me!" He is cowering on the floor, hiding his face in his hands, while the monkey sits on the counter, helping itself to a freshly baked curry puff.

"My cakes! My bakery! My reputation!" sobs Mr. Mani.

But Lal has not been a Mumbai postman for nothing. Granted, he has been on the job for only six months. But in that time he has dealt with rogues, ruffians, and pickpockets of all sizes and shapes—this one is not human, but it makes no difference.

"Hey!" Lal says to the monkey. "What do you think you are doing? You want to rob this fine bakery of its number one menu item or what?"

As he is talking to the monkey, Lal notices something that he has never noticed before. When he is dealing with rogues and ruffians, he stops stuttering. This is quite a realization. It makes him stand up taller. Then he thinks that perhaps it was that Mumbai postmaster who made him trip and stumble over his words.

The monkey chatters at Lal. This hill monkey does not know that it is supposed to be afraid of a Mumbai postman.

The monkey offers Lal a curry puff. Lal is so surprised that he sets the bag of pepper down on the counter and takes the curry puff from the monkey.

In a flash the monkey grabs the pepper bag.

The monkey shakes the bag. Fine pepper flies everywhere. The monkey begins to sneeze.

Now, pepper (freshly ground, from the pepper vines of the Blue Mountains) is a powerful thing. The monkey sneezes and sneezes from that fine pepper. It sneezes so hard it sneezes itself right out of the door, and all the way down the hill as well. It goes off to relay the message to all the other monkeys up and down those hills to stay away from that bakery forever.

"Oh-aah-bushku! Thank-choo!" sneezes Mr. Mani.

"No problem," says Lal.

"Oh, Lal," says Lila.

In the moments that follow, everyone is overcome by a round of grateful sneezing.

A man with a mauvish tint to his face has been watching the whole monkey episode with great interest. "Was that a movie scene?" he says now, muffling a sneeze with a large white handkerchief. "A movie scene or what, my darlings?" His face has now settled into a more even hue, quite close to the color of the flowers that Lal and Lila saw cloaking the hillside on the way up.

It is the mention of movies that jiggles Lal's

memory into place. He knows who this man is! It is Mr. Soli Dustup, to whom he delivered that Speed Post letter in Mumbai. He is about to tell him this, but he does not stand a chance in the avalanche of words from Mr. Dustup.

"Monkeys," says Soli Dustup, shaking his head. "If I'd thought of that two movie projects ago, I would be a rich man, I tell you." He sticks his hand out. "Soli Dustup, pleased to meet you. Mani, my gracious host, curry puffs all round."

Lal shakes the outstretched hand that swallows his own in its grip. "It's an honor to meet such a famous executive . . . ," he begins.

"In the movie business," Lila finishes for him.

"You are familiar with the movie business?" Mr. Dustup inquires.

Lal and Lila explain that they are merely fans. And that they are newly married and here on their honeymoon.

"And I . . . ," Lal begins.

"We . . . ," Lila adds.

"Oh, yes," says Lal. "We . . . well, that is to say . . ."

He finds he has forgotten what he meant to say. No matter, Lila takes over. She tells Mr. Dustup how nothing would please them more than to catch a glimpse, just a glimpse, of Dolly Singh, who is their very favorite movie star. They are humble people and they do not ask for much.

"Me too," says Soli Dustup, happy to find kindred spirits. "I have been trying to phone our Dolly for weeks, literally. Weeks. The blinking woman has stopped answering her phone, or the blinking number is on the blink, or what? Sit, sit, sit, those curry puffs will be here soon. They're out of this world."

Lal and Lila sit. Lal blinks, a little bewildered by this deluge of words. Mumbai postmen are used to fast talkers, but this man is a human flash flood.

"Here, let me give you my card," says Mr. Dustup.

Lal, in turn, notes down for him the telephone number of the hotel. "It's the hotel next to the tea and spices shop," he explains.

"What do you know?" says Mr. Dustup. "I'm in that same blinking hotel, Up in Arms or whatever it is. Well, well, well, always a pleasure to meet fans of our incomparable Dolly." He lowers his voice. "Mind you, she's a little temperamental. These stars. But I'll find her, I tell you, now that I have come so far. All the blasted way from Bombay." He tells them about his hair-raising trip. "But what to do? I have no car, so I have to trust myself to that same maniac driver. He'll be here very soon. Wish me luck, my friends."

And they do, they do.

Chapter Forty

Blooming Spirits

AS MR. MANI LISTENS to all this travel talk in his bakery, which is fragrant with fresh curry puffs and good chocolate, his heart is unexpectedly touched. He serves his customers their curry puffs. "Potatoes, onion, turmeric with a hint of chocolate, in a perfectly golden pastry crust," he says.

Blissful silence follows, interrupted only by murmurs of pure joy.

Many people come through Dreamycakes Bakery, and over the years Mr. Mani has stopped paying attention to them. They are just customers. They give him money. He gives them cakes and pastries and various other delicious offerings. A word or two, a smile, and they are gone. But these are fine people, Mr. Mani can see. He hopes he is lucky enough to see them again and again and again.

They are the kind of people he would like to count among his friends.

He hopes that Dolly Singh is happy to see Mr. Dustup. He would never say this to these kind souls, but the last time he saw that Dolly Singh person, she was a little—well, skittish. That is the word. Only a skittish person would have dashed a plate of curry puffs and chocolate cake so callously to the ground.

Lal brings out his wallet. Mr. Dustup says, "No, no, my treat!"

Lal and Lila express their gratitude.

"Think nothing of it," says Soli Dustup. "My pleasure purely. No blinking need for thanks at all."

They say good-bye to Mr. Mani.

"Come back," Mr. Mani tells them. "Come back for a fresh batch of curry puffs (potatoes, onion, turmeric with a hint of chocolate, in a perfectly golden pastry crust) or a slice of superfine chocolate cake anytime you are in the area."

He beams, quite dizzy from so much excitement. He wonders if someday he can expand his little Dreamycakes Bakery into a bigger bakery. He could get himself a van like that white Qualis he has seen parked at the medical clinic. He could race up and down the mountain roads, delivering his fine baked goods to happy customers. Why not?

It has been a long time since Mr. Mani dreamed in this way. He finds himself whistling smartly as he straightens his curtains. He looks out of the window and beams at the sight of this nice young couple, so well starched, walking off along Blue Mountain Road. And there now is the distinguished Mr. Dustup, a fillum studio bigwig, no less. Oh, it's enough to set anyone dreaming.

Dreaming makes Mr. Mani's spirits bloom like the purply blue kurinji flower.

Chapter Forty-one

Giving an Inch

PRIYA DROPS LETTERS one at a time into the red mailbox that stands outside the front door of the post office. It may look like an oversize fire hydrant, but it is a perfectly acceptable place to drop off your mail. The letters make a satisfying little thump when they land inside.

"Hey," says Priya. "Look."

"What?" says Dini. From habit she wonders if Dolly, perhaps, has come to the post office to mail a letter.

Priya points.

There is a peacock on the top step! Dini has only ever seen a peacock in a zoo before. All the other times she's been to India, she's visited cities where peacocks do not exactly roam around the streets. But here is one now, sitting on the step and shaking out its long, long tail.

Priya makes the exact noise that the peacock is making with its tail, a sound between the rustle of paper and the patter of rain on hard, dry ground. The peacock turns its head and looks at them. It utters a startled squawk. Priya squawks back at it. Dini tries too, but she starts laughing.

The peacock turns its head to look at them out of its other eye. It blinks, and Dini sees that its eyelids are white. Who ever knew a peacock's eyelids could be white? Blink-blink goes the white-eyelidded peacock. It obviously decides Dini and Priya are harmless, because it goes back to rustling its tail.

Dini tries to make that shivery paper-and-rain noise, and it does not come out sounding anything like that peacock's tail. It sounds only like a person making funny noises. Priya laughs, and Dini laughs too. One laugh leads to another, and soon they are both laughing very hard.

Is it the sound of peacock tail rustling that brings a man with very round glasses on his nose out of the post office? Or is it the sound of two girls laughing?

It is neither, it seems. The man pins a notice to the door of the post office. JOB! JOB! JOB! says the notice. APPLY WITHIN.

"Hello," says Dini.

"Hello," says the man. "Are you by some chance interested in working at the post office?" He peers at them through his round glasses and shakes his head in disappointment. "No, I suppose not. You're a bit on the young side."

"You need a postman?" Priya asks.

"Postal carrier, I like to call them these days," says the man with round glasses. "We must consider women also for this very important job. I had a most reliable carrier, but alas . . . Well, that's neither here nor there."

The peacock spreads its tail out as if it agrees completely. With an enormous shuffling and shivering of feathers, it sweeps it up into a big, round fan. The man with the glasses looks as if he is about to offer the postal carrier job to the peacock, but then he says to Dini and Priya, "If you know anyone who may want this job, please to let that person know. I'm the postmaster here, and I'm anxious to hire the right applicant, very soon."

Perhaps the peacock is disappointed, because it promptly walks away. It waddles across the road and disappears into some bushes. Its long and sweeping tail disappears after it. Soon all that is left is a faint, faint rustle, barely a whisper on the wind.

The postmaster disappears too, into the post office. Dini and Priya start to walk down the hill toward the shops on Blue Mountain Road.

Dini says, "I've never seen a peacock so close up."

"Me neither," Priya agrees. "And I'm Not going to make that Noise again because my Stomach still hurts from all that Laughing."

"Priya," says Dini. "I'm glad we can be friends."

"Me too," Priya says. "You know, I didn't really want to come Here because I had friends in Bombay and I didn't want to leave them."

"Me *too*," Dini cries. "I didn't want to leave my friend Maddie. But I did want to try and find . . . you know. . . ."

"You can say her Name," Priya says. "Dolly, you Mean."

Dini nods.

"He's ready to Talk to her," Priya says. "My parents Telephoned. I heard him telling Mummy that. She's his Big Sister, my mum. But it's Her. Dolly. She won't Give an Inch."

It is a comforting thought that Chickoo Uncle has a Big Sister to give him good advice. Dini has sometimes wished she had one, but no one asks kids for their preferences in such matters. "Not an Inch?" she says.

Priya nods. They both agree that's bad. "To patch up a Disagreement," Priya points out, "both Parties have to Give an Inch."

"At least," Dini agrees, waving at some kids who ride by, trilling their bicycle bells. "I wish I had my bike here," she says.

"There's a Bicycle Shop near the garage where you can Rent them," Priya says. "You should get one. We could Ride Bikes Together." Dini thinks that is a Brilliant Idea.

Before taking the bus back to Sunny Villa Estates, they stop at Dreamycakes for a rose petal milk shake.

"With or without chocolate?" says Mr. Mani.

"With," Dini says at the same time that Priya says, "Without."

"Righto," says Mr. Mani.

"Want to come for a Test-Drive tomorrow?" Priya asks Dini. "Veeran is going to put a New Battery in Chickoo Uncle's car. We're hoping That will Fix the Noise."

"Sure, I'll come," Dini says. She feels for Chickoo Uncle. She does. A broken heart *and* a noise in your car is a bit much.

"Wait just a minute, sir," Mr. Mani says, speaking to a portly man, quite out of breath, who has just come in.

Mr. Mani brings Dini and Priya their rose petal milk shakes, with chocolate and without. "There you are, young ladies," he says. "Enjoy."

"Are you okay?" Dini says to the new customer, who is now wiping his brow as though he has a fever.

He nods, breathing heavily.

His face is a little too purple, Dini thinks. Looks unhealthy. Someone should take this man to Mom's clinic for a quick check.

Chapter Forty-two

The Sound of an Aching Heart

THE REST OF THE DAY passes quickly, as happy days will. The next day too looks as if it is getting ready for happiness. Purply flowers are blooming along the side of the road. The sky is a superfine china blue, the leaves on the tea bushes sport a cheerful gloss. Anyone would think that this day is a dream come true.

Only one thing spoils it. The new battery that Veeran brought to Mr. Chickoo Dev's house and installed just this morning has not laid that terrible rattle to rest. All the way from Sunny Villa Estates and up the length of Blue Mountain Road on this test-drive with Chickoo Uncle at the wheel, the ugly rattle makes it impossible for anyone in the car to hear the birds singing, the cows mooing, or even the purry little engine of the just-out-of-warranty yellow electric car.

Clinkety-plinkety, goes the noise.

"What a racket," Chickoo Uncle says between clenched teeth. "It's going to drive me out of my mind."

Clunkety-blunkety-dunkety, goes the noise. Chickoo Uncle's shoulders droop. "I don't understand you," he says miserably, and it is evident that he is speaking to the car. "Veeran is a good mechanic—certified and all. He's torn out your engine and put it back again—fuses, motor, motor controller, and now batteries. Why, why, why?"

The car only rattles in reply.

"It's not singing anymore, is it?" Dini says.

"No," says Chickoo Dev. "It stopped singing a few days ago. Now it only rattles."

Dini can see right away that Mr. Chickoo Dev is not normally a tooth-clenching, shoulder-drooping kind of guy, but she can also see that he really loves this car. It is hard when you love two things equally well and you have to choose between them. Chickoo Uncle is so sad that Dini begins to wilt in sympathy.

Around them traffic thickens as they get to the busy part of Blue Mountain Road. Suddenly someone standing next to a white van waves at them. Chickoo Uncle brakes and eases to a stop on the side of the road.

"Hello, Mr. Chickoo Dev, Miss Nandini, Miss Priya," says a familiar voice.

It is Veeran. His mustache has gained extra-fine points on the ends. Veeran has news. "A big film studio executive," he says, "has come to Swapnagiri to meet Miss Dolly. I'm taking him there right now."

Chickoo Uncle dabs at his forehead with a big white handkerchief, even though it's nice and cool. Dini sees that he is flustered at hearing Dolly's name. That is what love can do. He parks the electric car and gets out. Dini and Priya follow.

"Why, that's Soli Dustup," says Chickoo Uncle in a small voice.

"You know him?" says Dini. "He's in all the *Filmi Kumpnee* articles. He's the guy who owns Starlite Studios."

"He is a nervous type," Veeran warns. "All the way here on the mountain road yesterday he kept telling me to slow down."

"Array!" shouts Mr. Soli Dustup, who has only

just spotted them and is making his way over. "Is it really you, Chickoo my friend?" He shakes Chickoo Uncle's hand so hard that Dini is afraid he will shake him right off his feet. "You have lost weight," he cries. "Your face looks wan and drawn. What a terrible blinking thing is heartache."

Chickoo Uncle teeters on his feet.

"Our Dolly," says Mr. Dustup, "has made life difficult for me, too, my friend."

Chickoo Uncle totters visibly.

"If I rang her blinking mobile once," says Mr. Dustup, looking as if his feet are starting to hurt again, "I rang it a hundred times. Ring-ring-ring, no answer. Ring-ring-ring, no answer. Has she fallen off a blinking cliff, I asked myself, has she disappeared into some picturesque waterfall or what?"

"Mo-bile?" Dini whispers to Priya.

"I think you call it a cell phone," she whispers back.

Dini clears her throat just as Mr. Dustup is saying for the third time, "Ring-ring-ring—"

"So," Dini says, trying to wiggle her way to the point, "are you going to see Dolly now?"

"Yes," says Soli Dustup, surprised at the interruption. "I would have gone earlier, but I was too exhausted, so I checked into a hotel room, some place called Up in Arms or something. Terribly hard beds, I tell you. Then I had to think, you see, to plan my strategy. But yes, I'm going to see her now."

"Can we come too?" says Priya. Good timing, before Mr. Dustup goes totally off script with those beds.

Dini sees that Chickoo Uncle is visibly distressed and is waving his hands at Priya but seems quite unable to speak.

"'We must turn the world right side up again,'" says Dini. She says it in her best dramatic voice because it is a fine line from MJTJ, a line Dolly uses to great effect when the police inspector is trying to figure out who she is and how he should deal with her.

Now it is Mr. Dustup who teeters and totters. "You know that movie," he whispers.

"Mr. Soli Dustup," Dini tells him, "I love that movie. I know every single line in it."

Mr. Dustup takes Dini's hands in both of his. He says, "Miss . . . I don't know your name, but let me tell you—you're a true fan, and what is more, you're a gift to a tired old filmi person like myself."

He staggers a little.

"Are you okay?" Dini asks.

"It's my feet," Mr. Dustup says weakly. "They are killing me. Too much walking. Too much. I should buy some more chocolate. I bought some of that superfine chocolate fudge yesterday, but alas, I ate it all."

Priya makes a sound like a flute playing.

"A very fine musical phrase that was," says Mr. Dustup appreciatively. "We should talk. There is possibly some scope for your talents in the sound-effects department."

Priya stays on task. Dini sees that she is that kind of person. Priya says, "Chickoo Uncle, you need to buy some chocolate."

"Oh," says Chickoo Uncle, dazed. "Oh yes."

Dini holds the door open, and they all go into the bakery. Mr. Mani is beside himself with delight at this influx of customers.

"My feet are happy, I tell you," says Soli Dustup to anyone who wants to listen, "just at the thought of riding in a car."

"What kind shall I buy?" says Priya's uncle, staring in bewilderment at the delectable array before him.

"I'd suggest the dark chocolate," says Mr. Mani.

"Righto," says Chickoo Uncle. Dini can see that Chickoo Uncle is doing a wise thing by putting himself into Mr. Mani's good hands.

"Maybe with rose petals?" says Mr. Mani.

Soli Dustup winces.

Chapter Forty-three

Shower of Silver

SOON TWO CARS make their way along Blue Mountain Road, past the shops and houses, past hillsides covered with dreamy blue flowers, and into the grounds of a place Dini has been before.

"Blue Mountain School?" Dini says. "Dolly's here? She's been here all along?"

Chickoo Dev nods his head. "The principal is a friend of hers," he says.

Of course! That explains the glimpse that Dini got of Dolly in the school movie. It explains the swishy way the principal got past Dini's question. A world-class subject changer, that principal, and now Dini can see why.

Dini wants to tell Chickoo Uncle that if he'd only told her this in the first place, it could have sped things up a bit. But then she thinks, That is just the way it is with plots. Tell too much too soon and it's all over. There's no story left. Besides, while coping with heartbreak, a person cannot hit the pause button to go off and tell other people small details like this. That kind of thing just ruins the fillum.

But here they are pulling up to the guesthouse on the school grounds, and Dini takes a deep breath. "It's now or never," she says, using one of Dad's nifty phrases.

Veeran says he'll wait outside with the cars. There is still some dialogue to be finalized, some plot turns to navigate. He is a true fan, and true fans get things like this.

Dini goes up to the door. This is it. Her Dolly moment. All right, so take one didn't work quite as planned, but that is why there is take two. She knocks on that door.

Dolly flings the door open and gasps. Even gasping she looks fabulous. Small, but fabulous.

Dolly lifts a hand questioningly. A ring flies off her finger and lands on the ground.

"it's you," Dolly says, and she's looking past Dini at Chickoo Uncle. No capital letters at all in that greeting. "why have you brought all these people here when you know i just want to be left alone."

That is not even a question, it is more of a complaint.

Dini picks up the fallen ring and hands it back humbly. This time they do not bump heads, which is a big improvement. "I'm sorry," Dini says. "If we're bothering you uselessly, we'll go away, but just give us ten minutes. Will you?"

Dolly nods. She lets them in, dropping a bracelet as she does so. The woman is a fountain showering silver all over. Dini picks up the bracelet and gives it back. This, perhaps, is what it means to be a grip.

"What I want to know," Dini says, "is why didn't you return Mr. Soli Dustup's call?"

"Calls," says Mr. Dustup, muscling into the conversation. "Many calls you didn't blinking return."

"What calls?" says Dolly. "My phone's been lost for weeks. No one's been able to phone me. That was the start of everything . . . going so terribly wrong." She wrings her hands. "Oh, it's the planet Mercury playing tricks on me!"

How well Dini knows that gesture! It is like in MJTJ when Dolly's character thinks it is all over.

"Oh, Dolly," Dini says, picking up a bangle that has just landed on the floor. A large bangle it is too. Quite heavy.

Mr. Soli Dustup says, "You never even phoned me back. You treated me . . . why, you treated me as if I were one of those pestering reporters from *Filmi Kumpnee*. You were star among my stars, Dollyji! Together we could have climbed the Dream Mountains of the fillum business. Why did you have to go and spoil it all?"

Dolly clasps her hands together, and it's right out of the MJTJ scene by the waterfall, the one just before everything is solved and everyone's heart is filled with complete joy. She says, "Kasme, vaade, sab toote pade hain!" And oh, Dini can feel the pang of those promises, promises, all lying about broken.

"Chickoo Uncle," Dini says. This is his cue.

But Mr. Chickoo Dev does not seem to be paying attention. He just stands there staring at Dolly as if he has never before seen such a dreamy-beautiful sight. Which is understandable, naturally, but Dini wants to say it does not do him any good. There is a time when a Person has to Act. Dini thinks even Priya would agree with her here.

But then she sees that Dolly is staring at Soli Dustup. Her mouth is open. Her jaw has dropped.

There is something about Swapnagiri, Dini decides, that makes this happen here, much more than you would expect in an ordinary day anywhere else.

Dolly says, "You phoned?"

"Ring-ring-ring!" Mr. Soli Dustup begins. "If I phoned once, I blinking phoned a hundred times. Ring-ring . . ."

Priya makes a sound like an exasperated monkey that has been duped out of its share of chocolate. "Stop him," she whispers.

Chapter Forty-four

Ring-Ring-Ring

IT IS CLEAR THAT SOLI could go on ad-libbing this dialogue for much too long. No sense of timing, that man.

Chickoo Uncle has found his words again. "I want to tell you—," he says timidly.

Dini hates to interrupt. She knows she should give the scene to the two people who need to be in the spotlight, but someone has to push the story along so it can even get there. She says, "Excuse me, Chickoo Uncle, but I have to ask. Dolly, when did you last see that phone?" She sounds like the police constable in MJTJ when he has the nerve to take Dolly herself in for questioning, but never mind. Some things cannot wait.

Dolly narrows her beautiful eyes. She puts a finger to her perfect chin, thinking.

"It was that day," she says, and she is looking at

Chickoo Uncle. "That day before we took your car down to the city." Her voice is not shattery exactly, but it's a little quivery.

This is it. The big plot point to this fabulous filmi scene. "Mr. Chickoo Dev, Chickoo Uncle," Dini says, and she is just about yelling from the excitement of it. "Can you go take the car seats out?"

"Car seats?" says Chickoo Uncle. His timing's getting better, even if he's not up on the direction of this scene. But then he gets it. He does. "Car seats?" he says again. "You don't mean . . ."

"Yes!" Dini shouts. "Now! Trust me."

Chickoo Uncle runs out of the Blue Mountain School guesthouse as if monkeys are after him.

Soon glorious, musical *clankety-clangs* break out, of car seats coming loose. In a few minutes Mr. C. Dev (Chickoo to his friends), of Dev Tea (Private) Limited, owner of Sunny Villa Estates, appears in the doorway. In one hand he is clutching a small silver phone. In the other is a bag of the finest dark chocolate with crushed rose petals.

"Yesssss!" Dini says, and Priya hisses along for company.

Dolly takes the bag with one hand and the phone with the other. She sets them both down. Then she picks up the phone. She flips it open.

"The battery is dead," she says, as if it is a thing of wonder.

Dini says, "You have songs for your ringtones, don't you?"

Dolly clutches the phone to her heart. "Yes," she says, "all songs from MJTJ."

"Ohhh!" says Chickoo Uncle. Dad would say that all is clear as the light of day.

"Exactly," Dini says. "Those mournful songs. That was the phone ringing."

"That was me," says Mr. Soli Dustup, "trying to phone you. Plug it in, plug it in. It'll be shipshape very soon. You have a charger?"

"Somewhere," says Dolly vaguely.

"Stars," says Soli Dustup fondly. "It's why they need people to manage them." He turns to Dini and says in a whisper, "It's not just the female leads, mind you. Those hero types are even worse."

Next Dolly peers into the bag. "Oh," she says in a trembly kind of way. "For me?"

Chickoo Uncle nods.

"I love-love-love crushed rose petal chocolate," says Dolly.

"I know," whispers Chickoo Uncle.

"I am so sorry for the terrible things I wrote to you," says Dolly. "So very, very sorry."

Chickoo Uncle runs a distracted hand through his mop of hair. "No, I am very, very sorry," he says, "for the terrible things *I* wrote."

"No, me," she says.

"Me, me," he replies. They could clearly go on for hours. Dini can tell that they really want to burst into song, a good filmi song like "Sunno-sunno! Dekho-dekho!" But in spite of this wanting to move the scene forward, they seem unable to stop repeating themselves.

There is so much that Dini wants to tell Dolly. But pacing is everything, and now is not the time for that. "Come on," she says to Priya. "Let's go outside and see what a yellow electric car looks like without its seats." Because when two people are on the brink of fixing past mistakes, it is really best for everyone else to simply get out of the way.

Priya makes a sound like an engine coming to life and heads for the door. Mr. Soli Dustup coughs. "You too," Dini tells him.

As Dini and Priya hurry Mr. Dustup out the door, Dolly and Chickoo Uncle seem to be cooing at each other like two of those pigeons you might see around the Gateway of India in Bombay that is now called Mumbai. Or around the Washington Monument.

Chapter Forty-five

Lal and Lila

"WHAT?" LILA SAYS. "You know him? That man with the purple face?"

"Shh," Lal says, looking round in case anyone has heard. "Yes. Something like that."

They are enjoying a tour of Swapnagiri in the Mountainview Tours minibus—operated by the nephew of the Open Arms owner. Lal has just told Lila about his business relationship, so to speak, with Mr. Dustup.

"Something? Nonsense." She is brisk and efficient, Lal's new wife. He is only just beginning to notice that. A commendable trait. "What a silly man," says Lila, "not to recognize you right away."

"I am only a postman," says Lal humbly.

"You are a very fine postman," says his loyal wife.

"Besides," Lal points out, "he was talking so much, he probably wasn't paying attention." It is easy to talk over Lal's humble voice. He does not say that, but it is true.

"Next time you see him, you should tell him," Lila says. "I'll help you."

Lal gazes in loving admiration at his wife. How lucky he is, he thinks, to be here with her in such a dreamy place. Look at the blue sky. Look at the matching blue of the hillsides, all covered with those beautiful little flowers. Look at the chocolate in that Dreamycakes Bakery.

His thoughts only intensify as the bus zigzags through the town. How kind a person is this minibus driver, who has taken such care to point out the local sights. The fine views. The two garages. The shops. Temple, church, mosque—one each. And that modest but heartfelt monument to the Indian postal system, the Swapnagiri Post Office.

"Do you think there could possibly be . . . ," Lal says to Lila as they drive past the post office.

"A job?" she says. "For you? Here? Why not?"

And on the spot they decide that if by some miracle there is a job opening in this post office, they will seriously consider leaving Mumbai that used to be called Bombay, for this most delightful of places.

Lal says, "But my mother . . ."

"She can come stay with us here," Lila says.

Lal thinks his mother would like that. She will have lots of room here to hang out the clothes that she starches so lovingly. In Bombay that is now Mumbai, the neighbors complain that she is using up too much room on the community clothesline on the eighth-floor terrace roof of their building.

Of course, the saffron in Lal and Lila's halva, the cashew nuts in their rice pulao, the icing on their cake, would be if they could just see Dolly.

What they do not yet know is that the saffron and cashew nuts, the icing, is waiting for them at the front desk of the Open Arms.

"A man phoned for you," says the woman at the front desk. "He talked very fast. Here is his number."

Lal phones the number. "What? Who is it?" Lila wants to know when he hangs up.

Lal shakes his head as if he can't believe what has just happened. "It's Mr. Soli Dustup," he says. "He says we should go to the Blue Mountain School guesthouse right now. There is someone there he wants us to meet."

❖ ❖ ❖

When Dini stops to think about it, coincidence is too simple a concept. It's much more complicated than that. It is as if all these people have arrived here at this moment for so many different reasons, and yet they are all meant to be here somehow. Their being here together makes this scene what it is.

Here, for example, just off the bus from town, is this couple in highly starched clothes. They may be getting off a local bus, but really, like Mr. Dustup, they have come to Swapnagiri all the way from Bombay that is now called Mumbai. As Dini tells everyone for the sixth time that day about how she first wrote to Dolly from Takoma Park, Maryland, the starchy-shirted man cries out, "That was you!"

"What was me?" says Dini, puzzled.

"You wrote a letter to Dolly Singh," he says, "Famous Movie Star, Bombay, is it not so?"

Dini has to admit that it is indeed so.

"I delivered it," he says modestly. "I put it most carefully into the proper occupant box. It was quite full at the time, so I was especially careful."

"Thank you," says Dini. She never thought she would meet the person who put that letter in

Dolly's mailbox with his own two hands. There is that coincidence thing again, and yet it is not random. There was no other way this story could have played out.

Lal's wife nudges him. "And you've also delivered…," she says, looking pointedly at the filmi executive person in the room.

Lal picks up his cue. "Yes, I delivered letters to Cuffe Parade flats for six months only, Mr. Soli Dustup."

"Array!" cries Mr. Dustup. "That is where I have seen you before." He waves his hands so excitedly that he seems to turn suddenly into a human windmill. "Who would believe it?" he cries, quite beside himself with emotion. "My blinking postman has come all the way to this Godforsaken place."

"Wow, wow, wow," Dini says. "It's a movie!"

Priya makes a soundtrack for opening credits.

"This whole thing could be a movie, could it not, my friends?" says Soli Dustup in a tizzy of delight.

Veeran the driver shakes his head from side to side in that way that means, Yes-yes-yes. Such things happen in the movies, and they happen in Swapnagiri. It is that kind of a place. Where else could a broken postal machine and car seats and a cell phone all figure in a story about making friends and healing broken hearts?

"I wish we didn't . . . ," Lal begins.

"Have to go back to Mumbai," Lila finishes for him.

And Dini knows. She knows that everything is now falling into place with that certain feeling you get from the endings of only the very best movies. All the story lines are coming together, pointing with a happy sigh in the right direction.

She says, "They're looking for a postal carrier here. At Swapnagiri post office. You should apply."

As is the custom in the finest of movies, Lal and Lila find themselves wiping tears of pure joy from their cheeks.

Finally, when all the stories have been told and all the hugs and tears have been hugged and shed, Mr. Soli Dustup lends Dini his cell phone, which is called a mobile in these parts, and Dini makes a phone call.

She hits all the zeros and ones that you need to enter to make an international call. She has to tell Maddie's mom, who answers the phone, that everything is just fine and there is nothing to worry about. It is just that she has the best-best-best news for Maddie, and sorry that it is 2 a.m., but sometimes time just will not wait.

When Dini says, "Maddie, I want you to say hello to Dolly Singh," Maddie's confusion turns to shock, then turns again into a shriek of pure delight. Dini hands the phone to Dolly. It is the kind of superfine moment that calls for a shot-reverse shot, where the camera switches from one face to another and back again, because how else can the audience get the big picture?

"Wowie, wowie, wowie," Maddie says to Dini moments later. "I talked to—Dini, did I just talk to—is this real? Tell me it's real, Dini."

"Yes," Dini assures her. "It's real, Maddie."

"You did it, you did it," Maddie says. "You found her, you found her. I knew you would. I knew you would." Maddie seems to need to repeat herself at this moment. Sometimes happiness has this effect.

Dini smiles, even though she knows that this is not an Internet video call and Maddie cannot see her smiling. Even though a smile is a silent thing, it is clear to her that on the other side of the world, at the other end of the phone connection, Maddie is smiling too.

Chapter Forty-six

Dancing with Dolly

IT TAKES DINI a while to fill Mom and Dad in. Even after they've been introduced to Dolly and heard the yellow car purr away, rid now of that dreadful noise, heard the happy news of Dolly's reengagement to Chickoo Uncle—even after all this, Mom and Dad keep asking Dini questions like "What did the noise in the car have to do with it?" and "Who's Lal?"

But eventually it is all sorted out, and even those in the audience who can't keep up with the fast pace of things have been brought, so to speak, up to speed.

And so the day dawns of the big celebration at Mr. Chickoo Dev's cottage number 1.

Mr. Mani has been working since daybreak to set up the refreshments.

Dini and Priya have been working with Dolly to

string flower garlands all around the outside of the house. Sampy has set up a green and silver arch over the gate. The whole place looks like a movie set.

"Keep an eye out for monkeys," whispers Mr. Mani, casting a suspicious eye about as he carries covered dishes into the lush green garden and sets them up on tables. "I have baked a most gigantic, superfine chocolate cake for the occasion. I have to take pictures to send."

"To Guinness World Records," breathes Dini.

"Why don't you take the cake inside?" Priya asks. "The monkeys can't get in."

"But I want to take its picture outside against this background," says Mr. Mani. "Simian villains." He grinds his teeth at the very thought of them.

"Don't worry," Dini says. "We'll keep them away from your cake."

Lal and Lila bring along a new friend. He is also Lal's new employer—the Swapnagiri postmaster. He seems to have been followed here by a peacock. It dances around the garden, shuffling its tail occasionally. Priya in turn echoes that sound, much to the peacock's surprise. It blinks at her with a Haven't-we-met? look on its face.

Lila has invited the tea-and-spices-shop man and his wife, who have offered her a job in the shop, which she has gladly accepted. They are talking to Mr. Mani about new and innovative ways to use their superfine pepper and other spices.

Dolly has invited Mrs. Balu, the principal of the Blue Mountain School.

"You," says Mrs. Balu, "are the young lady who wrote that most impressive essay that was format-ted like a movie script."

Dini admits that was her.

"You," says Mrs. Balu, "are a talented young lady. We are most happy to have you in our school."

"And my friend Priya," Dini says. Priya makes her flute sound, followed by drums.

"You," says Mrs. Balu, "are very impressive. A human sound system. Our drama teacher will be thrilled. You know, I always find that the new school year is so exciting." And she goes off, rubbing her hands, to get herself some of those curry puffs with potato and onion and a hint of chocolate.

Mom has invited all the doctors from the clinic, who in turn have invited all their patients, who in turn have brought their husbands and parents and in-laws. And the babies! There are babies everywhere, gurgling and cooing and climbing all over the furniture and getting underfoot and babbling at the goats, but no one minds in the least.

Yes, indeed, goats. The goatherd has brought his precious animals. Someone told him that there was going to be a party, and that no one would mind if his darlings did a little cropping of the grass outside cottage number I. The goatherd has also brought a handful of kurinji blossoms. "Rare good luck," he says, giving Dini one. "They bloom only every twelve years."

"What shall I do with it?" she asks.

"Here," Mom says. "Let me." And she tucks it into Dini's hair and pins it in place. It has a mild scent, a little lemony. It makes Dini want to dance.

"Twelve years," Dini says. Every twelve years. She is not quite twelve yet, but she will be by the end of the year. "That means the last time they bloomed . . ."

"Was the year you were born," Mom says.

It's a fabulous fact. How incredible that the flower bloomed last, and Dini was born, and Dolly made her fillum debut, all in that one year.

At last, at long and lovely last, Dini tells Dolly that fabulous fact. "That was a pretty starry year, huh?"

"Superbly stellar," says Dolly. She gives Dini an effusive rose-scented hug, showering her with bits of jewelry, and goes off to greet her guests.

And what a milling, thronging crowd of guests!

Veeran, Mala, and the baby, Inji the sausage dog and his owner, Mrs. Chellappa. Local celebrities, TV people, shopkeepers, tea pickers. One way or another, the entire population of Swapnagiri is at this party.

Is there anyone missing? Yes, and here she comes, with a recording device and a microphone, hurrying toward the joyful crowd. "Roopa Dalal, from the 'News 'n' Views' column of *Filmi Kumpnee*," she says, all out of breath. "Is there any chance of an exclusive interview?"

But she is too late. "Dance, meri jaan," says Dolly, and she grabs Roopa Dalal by both hands and hauls her, protesting, up the ladder to the roof. Up the ladder goes Roopa, her recording device bumping along behind her. And soon there is Dolly leading the entire company in a giant extravaganza of a group dance on the roof of cottage number I, Sunny Villa Estates. People and goats, peacock and babies, everyone is stepping along.

Chan-chan-chan, go Dolly's silver anklets.

Dhoom-taana-dhoom, go the drumbeats. Wait. There are no drums. That is just Priya being a one-girl sound-effects crew.

"Come on, Mom, Dad, Chickoo Uncle," says Dini. And up the ladder they all go, following Dolly in this great big dance scene. A grand finale, as filmi people would put it. Mrs. Chellappa's little dog, Inji, barks in time. Even the miniature green birds that hang upside down in the bottlebrush trees are flapping their wings in time to the beat.

Soon the dance has been danced, and the extravaganza is over. The dancers all come down from the roof with thudding pulses and happy hearts.

But wait! There's more to come. In the elegantly sprawling garden, a table has been set up. On that table, Mr. Mani has just unveiled the most gigantic chocolate cake that anyone has ever seen.

Chapter Forty-seven

Listen-Listen, Look-Look

"EVERYBODY SAY, 'HI, DOLLY!'" cries Roopa Dalal, the *Filmi Kumpnee* reporter.

Everyone gathers around Mr. Mani's cake.

"Hi, Dolly!" everyone cries.

But . . . but . . . but . . .

Between the dance number and the happy ending, all too often, one last rock of conflict can, and often does, tumble down even the most idyllic movie hillside. Put another way, there is a nifty saying that Dini's dad is fond of, that every cloud has a silver lining. He uses it to point out that one must always be hopeful.

Suppose for a moment that this is true. Then it must also be true that many silver linings also have clouds, or else why would smart people like Dini's dad believe in them? This day's silver lining, which is no doubt caused by Dolly shedding her jewelry as she dances, now proceeds to show its cloud.

An excited chatter sounds from the trees. Some-one who has not been invited to the party is here. Many someones, in fact, all of them with bright eyes and long tails.

Mr. Mani freezes.

"Oh no!" says Priya.

"Oh no!" whimpers Mr. Mani. "It is the curse of Dreamycakes Bakery. Oh, my poor great-grandfather." He covers his face with his hands.

"Ayyoyyo!" cry Veeran and Mala.

"Hai, hai," say Lal and Lila. They look at each other. They do not need to speak the thought in both their minds. There is no bag of pepper handy to drive these monkeys away.

"Oh, what a sad tale," sobs Mr. Mani. This is dreadful. These monkeys really do reduce him to a weeping panic.

Sampy scowls. "We should send you to America," he says to those monkeys. "They will teach you some manners over there."

"Those monkeys really take the cake," says Dad.

"Shh," says Mom.

Dad says, "Sorry. Just slipped out."

But what will become of Chickoo Uncle and Dolly's reengagement party, not to mention Mr. Mani's pictures for the Guinness World Records company, if these simian villains do take the cake?

Dini steps up. Someone has to. "Just go ahead and take their pictures too," she says. "Why not? Look. We have goats and a peacock—why not some monkeys, too?"

The monkeys stare. Perhaps they are not used to such invitations.

"Hey, you!" Lal says to the monkeys. "Come on. What are you waiting for?"

The monkeys listen-listen.

"Oy, monkey darlings," says Mr. Soli Dustup, "just think of this as a blinking audition. You could be in *Sunny Villa: The Movie*."

The monkeys look-look. Then, in a series of moves that would probably have turned Dolly's body double in MJTJ green with envy, they leap down from the trees and gather around the cake right along with the people, not to mention the goats and the peacock.

"Sunno-sunno," Dolly sings, and the entire company joins in. "Dekho-dekho." *Click-click-click*, goes
Roopa the reporter's camera! It is, as Dini's dad
might have said, if anyone could have heard him
over the racket, a sight for sore eyes.

Dini looks around at everyone gathered together

on this picture-perfect day, with the sun going down and the tea-gardens settling into the evening.

"Can you give me copies of those pictures?" Dini asks Roopa. "So I can send them to my friend Maddie?"

"No problem," says the reporter. "I'll send them to you by e-mail. We at *Filmi Kumpnee* love to share with fans all over the world."

Dini sighs. In her mind those pictures zip into the computer in cottage number 6. She'll print one of them out and ask Dolly if she'll sign it for her. "To Maddie," in green glittery ink. Then Dini will take it to the post office, and that nice postmaster, who is here today with his friend the peacock, will tell her how many stamps it needs. Lal himself, the new starchy-uniformed letter carrier for Swapnagiri, will help send that picture on its way to Maddie.

There are many kinds of sighs. The one Dini

sighs now is wrapped in contentment. That word that Dolly used in her special-features interview. "Surreal." Dini didn't get it at first, but it was the word that made her think of the Dini Meets Dolly plot plan in the first place. Now Dini gets that word. Completely and totally gets it.

It's not always a bad thing when things turn surreal. It's what life can be sometimes. Strange and weird, beyond real.

Everything that's happened here in this Dream Mountain place has been a bit surreal, a kind of shimmery, dreamy version of real. Like a fillum, only better.

Don't miss the grand sequel!

Dini and Maddie—and even Dolly!—are back. . . .
But this time you'll find them in the good old U. S. of A.

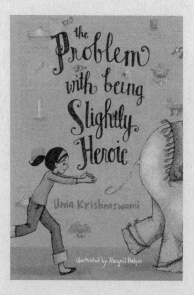

KHSV

DINI AND MADDIE, best friends forever, dance around the room in swirls of green and silver, silver and green. Green and silver scarves, skirts, pants, tunics, shoes, and sandals lie scattered all over Maddie's room. Stripy notebooks and pens are heaped on the desk, along with a jumble of jewelry.

Dini is a fan of Dolly Singh, Bollywood movie star extraordinaire, whose signature colors, as everyone knows, are green and silver, silver and green. Dini is a Dolly fan, so Maddie is with Dini. That's how best friends are.

Faster and faster they go. One. Two. One-two-three. One. Two. Back-two-three and forward-two-three and one. Two.

A bangle clatters to the floor. "Oops," says Maddie.

"Just like Dolly," says Dini. They laugh together.

It's true. Dolly does drip jewelry, literally, wherever she goes. She will shortly be scattering her fabulous baubles right here in the Washington, D.C., area, when she and her own true love, Mr. Chickoo Dev, arrive for the American premiere of Dolly's latest, greatest movie, *Kahan hai Sunny Villa?* or *Where Is Sunny Villa?* KHSV for short.

Dini quits dancing to hand Maddie's bangle back to her. "Maddie," she says, "I've got something for you." She flings the trailing end of the scarf over her shoulder and digs in her suitcase. "I meant to give it to you yesterday."

A shoe flies out, and a green stripy sock. "Where is it?" Dini says.

"Where's what?"

"This. Look!"

Maddie looks. Maddie screams.

The door bursts open. It's only Gretchen, Maddie's mom. "Everything okay?" she says, looking around the room. Seeming to satisfy herself that no one has died, she exits.

Maddie rolls her eyes. Dini shrugs. Of course everything is okay. Screaming is completely justified.

Dini's gift is a photograph, signed and inscribed in glittery ink by Dolly herself: "Salaam-namaste to Maddie, my dearest friend and fan. Hugs and kisses, Dolly Singh."

"Oh!" says Maddie. "Salaam-namaste! Am I saying it right?"

Dini's not always certain how to say things right in Hindi, but little things like language shouldn't get in the way of enjoying a really good fillum, what true fans call these movies. "I knew you'd love it," Dini says.

"Is that your house?" says Maddie, looking closely at the picture of Dolly. She's dancing in front of a house whose funny-looking shutters give it a blinky look.

Your house. The words halt the moment and stretch it like a rubber band. The moment gathers itself and moves on, but it leaves Dini a bit stunned. "Um, yes," she says.

The different places in her life are mixing and merging instead of staying firmly on the ground as places are supposed to do. Here, for instance, is Takoma Park, Maryland, a hop and a skip by Metrorail from Washington, D.C., the nation's capital.

And there is Swapnagiri, the little town in the Blue Mountains of south India whose name means "Dream Mountain," and Dini knows that it doesn't disappoint. It's where Dini now lives with her parents, and will live until Mom's grant ends and they all come back to . . . to here.

Here. There. Here. They swirl and whirl in Dini's mind. She tries to shake off the dizzying effect. There is no time for dizziness.

Maddie is talking about how she can't wait to see all those amazing tea-gardens and houses and whatnot in the movie and how dreams can come true, never mind what anyone says, and isn't that just soooo . . . ? She props Dolly's picture up on her bookcase. "There, how's that?"

"Perfect," says Dini automatically.

It is perfect. It is. Dolly looks on top of the world up there, between a penny jar and a tangle of beads.

Maddie dances some whirly-twirly steps that she ends on a sideways freeze with both arms stuck out. She looks like a person who has stepped out of an ancient Egyptian tomb painting.

No-no-no, Dini thinks. That is not it. Not at all.

"I wonder if we find just the right music . . . ," she

says, trying to sound helpful and hopeful. She turns the volume up, so that Dolly's voice comes pouring into the room. It's a glorious voice, even in this demo audio cut from the movie soundtrack.

"Haan-haan-haan, nahin-nahin!" sings Dolly in a catchy melody that underscores a stirring moment of decision. Dolly's songs have a way of cutting right to the heart of Dini's own feelings, yes-yes-yes all mixed up with no-no.

Maddie circles around Dini waving a rainbow stripy scarf over her head with both hands. The gold accents on the scarf blur as the Egyptian person step-turns into a belly dance of some kind. "How's this?" Maddie demands. "Am I getting it? Close?"

"Nahin-nahin!" Dolly sings.

"Try it this way." Dini shows her how to make V-shaped designs on the floor with one foot, then the other, before leaping forward with a hand extended, palm out.

Then back and around
      and one more loop,
           and back and around
      and one more loop, and again

and again, just
one more loop
and—hands together—
sliiiide
to a
stop.

"See?" She is breathless from it. "Want to try?
You have to repeat and repeat and slide-slide-slide.
It's a pattern." She has studied every single dance
move in a dozen Dolly movies to come up with this
combination.

For a brief time, there is only the sound of ankle bells and bangles.

This dance sequence needs to be exciting, and dreamy wonderful. But it also needs to be Dolly-ish, which means no Egyptian-tomb-painting steps.

As they go down to dinner, help Maddie's mom put plates out, and pour juice and pick a salad dressing, Dini frets. She can see that Maddie is worried too.

"Did I do it wrong?" asks Maddie anxiously, blocking her mother's attempts to add sunflower seeds to her salad.

"No," Dini says, although she wants to cry, No-no-no! Or does she mean yes-yes?

It is possible that some of Dini's confusion comes from traces of that odd feeling that travelers know as jet lag, which turns night into day and wakefulness into sleep. Maybe some of it is also because her family is scattered about like bits of Dolly's flying finery. Dad came from India with Dini on that long-long-long flight, but he's staying with a friend who runs a B&B a couple of blocks away. Mom, of course, is back in India taking care of the health and wellness of women in her little clinic.

All of which makes perfect sense. So what's the problem? Dini takes a moody bite of chicken salad and lettuce sandwich with some kind of mustardy spread that Maddie's mom has made from scratch.

She's been looking forward to seeing Maddie again! To planning this dance. To being here for the grand premiere of KHSV. Nowhere in that looking forward was there even a hint of this mixed-upness. She tries to recover a squirt of mustard spread that has escaped from her sandwich, but it splats hopelessly onto the tablecloth.

IRRESISTABLE FICTION
from Edgar Award–winning author
FRANCES O'ROARK DOWELL!

FALLING IN

THE SECRET
LANGUAGE OF GIRLS

THE KIND OF FRIENDS
WE USED TO BE

THE SECOND LIFE
OF ABIGAIL WALKER

DOVEY COE

WHERE I'D LIKE TO BE

CHICKEN BOY

SHOOTING THE MOON

Atheneum

ATHENEUM BOOKS *for* YOUNG READERS
KIDS.SimonandSchuster.com

"Eva's spirit soars."

—Karen Hesse,
Newbery Medal–winning author of *Out of the Dust*

If I were Joan of Arc,
I could defeat the Demon Snag myself
with a shining sword.
But I am only Eva of the Farm,
armed with a shining imagination
that makes me run home fast.

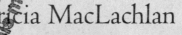